Chance and the Butterfly

Chance and the Butterfly

Maggie de Vries

ORCA BOOK PUBLISHERS

National Library of Canada Cataloguing in Publication Data
De Vries, Maggie.
Chance and the butterfly

"An Orca young reader"
ISBN 1-55143-208-0

I. Title.
PS8587.E895C52 2001   jC813'.54   C2001-910949-0   PZ7.D497Ch 2001

Library of Congress Catalog Card Number: 2001092680

Orca Book Publishers gratefully acknowledges the support of
our publishing programs provided by the following agencies:
the Department of Canadian Heritage, The Canada Council
for the Arts, and the British Columbia Arts Council.

Cover design by Christine Toller
Cover illustration by Don Kilby
Interior illustrations by Cindy Ghent
Printed and bound in Canada

IN CANADA
Orca Book Publishers
PO Box 5626, Station B
Victoria, BC Canada
V8R 6S4

IN THE UNITED STATES
Orca Book Publishers
PO Box 468
Custer, WA USA
98240-0468

03 02 01 • 5 4 3 2 1

For my niece Jeanie, who loved this book
even before it was done.

For my nephew Ben,
who loves creatures of all kinds.

And in memory of their mother,
my sister Sarah, who loved us all.

I would like to thank Cheryl Wainwright and
her students for welcoming me into their classroom
and helping me to get the caterpillar and butterfly
details just right. Any errors that remain are,
of course, mine alone.

Chapter One

"Let's go, let's go, let's go," Chance shouted. "The butterflies are coming today."

He jumped off the couch, scattering papers and books and sending to ruin the Lego tower he had started the night before. No time to stop. Mark would be mad when he found his school books on the floor, but at least the tower belonged to Chance. His to build. His to smash.

Hair uncombed, shoelaces dragging, Chance flew to the door and flung it open.

"The butterflies are coming, the butter-flies are coming," he chanted, his voice drowning out even the cries of that sad baby that Angie, his new foster mother, was feeding in the kitchen.

"Yes, Chance, I'm right with you," said his foster father, Doug. He gathered up Chance's lunch bag and backpack and followed him out the door.

Then they had to wait in the car for Mark … just as they had waited every morning since Chance had come to stay here, three weeks ago.

"I don't see why we always have to go so early, Dad," Mark groaned as he finally swung into the front seat. He ignored his younger foster brother, just as he had on the last fifteen school-day mornings. Chance knew, though, that Mark would not forget those books on the floor.

Chance hunched down in the back seat. He concentrated his thoughts on the life cycle of the butterfly. Eggs, larvae (those were the caterpillars), chrysalides, butterflies. Eggs, larvae, chrysalides, butterflies.

Was it so terrible that Mark ignored him? He had stayed in houses with other kids before, not foster kids, kids who belonged there, like Mark did. And they had ignored him before. And done much worse. Eggs, larvae, chrysalides, butterflies.

Every traffic light was red on the route to school, and Doug insisted on driving just below the speed limit the whole way as usual. Then, when they got there, Chance couldn't go in anyway, because it was nowhere near a quarter to nine.

Mark took off for the gravel field behind the school. The grade fours and fives always played soccer there before the bell.

Chance stood right by the entrance nearest his class for the whole time. Doug waited over by the bicycle stand, keeping an eye on him.

"The butterflies are coming," Chance reported to any children who came near enough to hear him. But even the kids in his own class just shrugged their shoulders and moved on. Didn't they care? The kids in this school were no different from kids in any of the other schools.

But at least here he was going to be part of something. He had left one school two days after the chicken eggs had been placed under the warm hatching lights. He had arrived at another two weeks after a brood of ducklings had been taken to a nearby farm. Here, for the first time, his timing was perfect. On Chance's first day in Ms. Samson's class, they had just been starting to learn all about the life cycle of Painted Lady butterflies. This time he was going to see it through.

Others in the class might not listen, but every word that Ms. Samson said about butterflies, Chance heard. Every picture that she showed, he pored over. The written words worked themselves into tangles and defeated him, but everything that he could learn about butterflies, he took right in deep. Not only was he going to be here until butterflies were flying around in the classroom, he was going to be an expert.

Now, as Chance waited for the bell, Ralph, a boy from his class, tried to budge in front of him. Chance elbowed him in the stomach. Ralph grunted, but did not take action. He wandered off, holding his belly.

Would he tell? Chance wondered briefly. Another lunch at the office? Another talk with the principal?

Only three weeks and already Chance knew every bit of Mrs. Laurence's office and every one of her tactics for dealing with unruly children.

"The butterflies are coming," he muttered one more time under his breath.

Chapter Two

The bell rang and Chance jumped, startled.

For the second time that morning, he flung open a door. For the first time ever, he beat everyone else into the classroom. Not even Ms. Samson was there yet. As the others spilled into the room behind him, Chance searched. He was quiet now, wanting to make the discovery himself.

Nothing in the room was different, except for a square cardboard box sitting on the round table. It had red and white labels on the sides. Chance could make out the word "live," but none of the others. The box had been opened and the top tucked closed again.

Still no sign of the teacher. It was easy to pull the box open and reach inside, among the foam chips. He had a heavy container in his hand and was peering through its clear plastic sides at some muddy greenish substance when he was interrupted.

"Chance, what are you doing? Put that down!" The voice sliced across the room, not too loud, but clear as clear.

Chance rarely listened to teachers' angry voices. In fact, most of the time he didn't even hear them until it was far too late. But something in Ms. Samson's voice today reached him. He set the container back in the box and stepped back from the table.

Ms. Samson crossed the room quickly, put her hand gently on Chance's shoulder and steered him toward the cloakroom to put away his bags and his coat. Then she lifted the box and headed for the story corner.

"Get your things put away and join me on the carpet, boys and girls," she said. "I have something exciting to share with you."

Chance made sure that he was sitting

right in front of her knees. Ms. Samson lifted a plastic cup from the box, exactly the same as the one that Chance had been looking at, with a white lid, and the same greenish stuff inside, but only in the bottom.

"What do you think these are?" she asked as she held it high.

A lot of tiny dark things were on the inside of the plastic sides. They looked kind of wriggly.

"Caterpillars!" the class called out in unison. A couple of voices said "larvae" instead. Ms. Samson seemed pleased.

"Hands up for this next question," she said. "Do you think the caterpillars will always be caterpillars?"

That was silly, Chance thought. "No. They'll become butterflies," he called out. Ms. Samson ignored him and called on Martha, who was holding her hand up in the air. She was sitting, legs neatly crossed, right beside him. "No. They'll become butterflies," Martha said.

Chance was hemmed in on all sides. He shifted in his spot, tried to gain himself a little space.

"Don't bother your neighbors, Chance," Ms. Samson said. "That's right, Martha," she went on. "As caterpillars, their only job is to eat and eat and eat to get lots of energy so they can turn into butterflies. Do you know, boys and girls, that if a baby could grow as fast as some kinds of caterpillars, that baby would be bigger than a bus by the time she was four weeks old."

Chance's brain reeled. "Then how big would the baby be by now, in grade three?" he asked eagerly, flipping onto his knees to see better how tiny they were now.

Half a dozen voices complained immediately.

"Sit down flat, Chance. And put your hand up," Ms. Samson said.

Chance collapsed onto his bottom and threw his hand into the air. He rattled off the question again. Of course, that wasn't exactly what she wanted, but it was so hard to wait, and his question was so important.

"Next time, wait for me to call on you, Chance," Ms. Samson said.

Chance gritted his teeth. Why did she

have to do this every single time? Why could nothing ever just happen?

But at least she answered the question. If the baby grew by the size of a bus every month, then they just needed to know how many months there were up until grade three. Together they worked it out. The baby would be about as big as one hundred and fifteen buses, since they were near the end of the year. Wow! The children gazed at the little caterpillars with great respect.

Still, Ms. Samson pointed out that larvae don't keep growing for seven years. They only have a month or so to grow in outdoors, and they grow even faster in the classroom. Not like us. We have twenty years to grow. We can take our time.

Then Ms. Samson explained again all the steps that the larvae would go through to become butterflies. At first, Chance listened carefully for new information, but they had already made a booklet that included everything she was telling them. So it wasn't long before his body started

to wriggle. He had never discovered anything that would keep him still once that
had started to happen. His teachers thought
he didn't try. They were wrong.

Ms. Samson looked down at Chance and
ordered him back to his desk. He scrambled on all fours through the group of cross-
legged children, not caring how many sides
he jabbed or fingers he trod on. Then he
took a roundabout route across the room,
clomping his feet as he walked. She spoke
to him again, more sharply this time. His
shoulders slumped and his eyes rolled. He
was going, wasn't he? Nothing he did was
ever good enough for anybody. He scraped
his chair on the hard floor pulling it out,
and then he shuffled it in, making as much
noise as he could. This time Ms. Samson
ignored him.

So Chance didn't get to press some food
into one of the little caterpillar containers
like everyone else. He didn't get to watch
Ms. Samson pick the caterpillars up one
by one with something she called a sort-
ing brush, just a little paintbrush as it turned

out, and place them one to a container on top of the food. And even though it was Chance's week as classroom helper, he didn't get to help her hand the containers out.

Martha did.

Each time Ms. Samson placed a caterpillar in its tiny cup, Martha handed the container, a lid and a magnifying glass to the next in line. One by one, every child in the class but Chance settled down to examine a tiny creature.

Over and over, Chance kicked his desk leg. Ms. Samson took forever to finish, but finally all the children were seated, chatting away about what they were doing. The teacher took the last container off the table, settled the last caterpillar into it, snapped a lid on and headed in Chance's direction, magnifying glass in hand. Chance kept his eyes moving and his leg kicking. He fixed his gaze on everything in the class that was not human, willing his teacher to go away and leave him alone.

She pulled up a chair and put the container on his desk.

"Let's look at this together, Chance," she said.

His shoulders were up around his ears, and his foot kicked one more time and then again. If she thought he wasn't mad, she was wrong. He was mad still, mad that he never got a chance, mad that everything had to happen somebody else's way. Never his.

But the caterpillar was right there and the magnifying glass was at his fingertips. So Chance looked. Then he looked some more. He saw the beautiful pattern of white spots and little stripy lines on the larva's back. He saw the tiny hairs sticking up all over its body. He saw its six little feet. As he gazed, the little creature became his. He would feed it. No, he would feed HER, protect her and watch her grow wings.

He looked up at Ms. Samson and grinned. "She's amazing," he said softly.

"Yes, she is. Especially when you think that she has everything she needs inside her to become a butterfly. The only other thing she needs is that food in there."

"Yeah," Chance said. He reached into his desk and rooted around. Bits of paper drifted out and a couple of broken pencils fell to the floor. The desk tipped. Ms. Samson's hand shot out and stopped the small container just as it was about to slide to the floor.

"Careful, Chance," she said. "What are you looking for?"

"A felt," he said. "I want to put my name on. So I'll know which is mine." He looked at his teacher. Her face spelled that familiar word, no. His face fell.

"All the caterpillars belong to all of us," she said. "That way if anything happens to one, we'll all still have others. I kept just the right number, twenty-six, for our class. The grade fours are going to keep an eye on the rest, but I don't want everyone claiming caterpillars for themselves."

Chance's chin thrust out; he sat and stared at his desk. Ms. Samson touched him briefly on the shoulder as she stood and swung her chair back into its spot at the round table at the back of the classroom. Chance could almost feel his skin twitch where she had touched him. She said "no" and then she patted him. What did she think he was, a puppy?

"Could you finish up, please, everyone?" she said. "Within five minutes all the caterpillars need to be on the work-in-progress shelf and the magnifying glasses need to be put away."

A few children got up and put their containers away. Chance watched. They were putting them in a jumble. He would never be able to pick his out again in that mess. And even if he put it somewhere else, it was sure to get found and moved. No. This one was his.

He thought for a long moment. He wasn't allowed to mark the container, but there had to be a way. There had to be. He wasn't allowed to mark it so she could see, or so anyone else would know. Making sure that Ms. Samson was not looking, he reached into his desk and felt around until his hand met his scissors. He tugged the lid off, took a quick look in at the little caterpillar. She was curled up in the bottom. Still as still. Scared, he thought. She needed to get to her spot away from all the noise.

Slowly, the scissors and the lid came together. One false move and he'd slice that lid right in half. Then he'd be in trouble! The first cut went all right. Now he just had to make another cut that met up with it. The scissors were small and dull. His thumb was thick and wanted to twist the scissors around the wrong way. And he had to hold everything right in his lap so no one would see. There! He made the second cut. A tiny triangle of plastic fell away. He snapped the lid back on. Yes. It still stuck.

He shoved the scissors out of sight and looked up to see Ms. Samson approaching his desk once again.

"Make sure the lid's on tight, Chance," she said, looking past him to check on the rest of them, "and put it over with the others." Then she turned back to the class. "Time for a math drill," she said. "Six times tables today."

Chance placed his caterpillar at the back of the shelf where she would be safe. He had got three out of twenty on the last math drill. When Ralph had gloated about getting the only A+, Chance had drawn thick black lines across Ralph's test. That had been the first time he had eaten his lunch outside Mrs. Laurence's office. Today was different. Today he could get one out of twenty and he wouldn't care.

His caterpillar was getting ready to grow.

Chapter Three

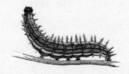

Dinner was casual in this new foster house. In the last one, the whole family had sat down at the dinner table every night and stared at each other. Here, Mark, who was their son, not their foster son, often took his dinner into the den. Angie set herself up at the kitchen table to feed that sad baby, as Chance called her to himself. Doug and Angie didn't eat until later when the baby was asleep, if she fell asleep. And there didn't seem to be any good place for Chance to eat his dinner, at least not after that first night.

The baby's name was Louise. Her mother had left her at the hospital after she was born. She had been sick and had to stay in the hospital for a long time. Then a family had adopted her. But she had been too sad for them. They had wanted a happy baby. And so they had given her back. After that Angie and Doug had taken her in as a foster child. Two months later they took Chance in too.

Louise was still sad. She cried all the time. She screamed and screamed. She screamed in the nighttime and in the daytime. She screamed in her crib and in her highchair and in Angie's and Doug's arms. Chance had a pretty good idea about why she was so sad. After all, he knew all about being abandoned and being given back. He was glad that Angie and Doug had kept Louise. They held her tight, wrapped in her blanket. They sang to her and talked to her.

Sometimes they seemed tired. Sometimes they even snapped at him or at Mark. But they never seemed to think of sending anybody back.

On that first day, a Saturday, his caseworker had dropped him off in the afternoon. She had come into the house for a few minutes, and had offered to stay longer, but he had brushed her away. "I'm okay," he had mumbled.

She had looked at him hard for a moment. "I'll be checking in next week," she had said. Then she had gone.

The house was quiet that afternoon. The baby was napping for once, and Mark was at some kind of sports event. Mark had wanted to be here to meet Chance, Angie said, but his coach was strict and couldn't spare him. Chance knew she was lying. The sons and daughters of foster parents never wanted him or any other foster kid around.

"We thought that maybe it would be easier for you to get to know us gradually, grown-ups first. And Louise," Angie said. Her smile was so big and warm that Chance was almost taken in. Almost. "You'll meet Mark tonight at dinner," she went on. "We're roasting a chicken to celebrate. I even cleared the table in the dining room, so we can have dinner together for once!"

Angie did seem nice. So did Doug. They showed him through the house, especially his room, where they put his bags. Then they led him into the kitchen and doled out milk and cookies. But his head felt stuffy and swollen, heavy on his shoulders. And pain ran up and down his back and legs. They didn't know him yet. This was just another in a long line of houses and apartments, of smiling grown-ups with milk and cookies. Those smiles never lasted more than a few weeks.

"Could I go to my room?" Chance said, his eyes on the table.

"There are lots of puzzles and crayons and games, tons of Lego, in the front room. You could take your cookies in there if you like," Doug said, his voice coaxing. Chance didn't have to look up to know that he was giving Angie a worried look.

"I just want to go to my room," Chance repeated. He knew that he sounded stubborn, that he was supposed to be grateful, to smile back. His caseworker, June, was always telling him those things. But he didn't have a smile in him.

"All right," said Angie. "Take some of these along. You must be starving," she added, folding his fingers around two enormous oatmeal cookies. Chance was not hungry. His throat felt as if it was full of rapidly hardening cement, but he took the cookies.

He froze halfway up the stairs as a horrible wailing poured forth from one of the bedrooms, the room that Angie and Doug had not shown him on their tour. "That's the baby's room," they had said. "She's napping." He had not known then what a miracle that nap was.

Angie came up the stairs behind him. "Well, I guess she's awake," she said lightly as she passed him. "I hope her racket won't bother you too much." The wailing turned to screaming, screaming that did not die down when Angie went into the bedroom. Keeping as far from the baby's door as he could, Chance made his way to his own bedroom.

Closing the door behind him, he stood and looked.

He was in a small room with a big window

right in front of him. The curtains were open, revealing a few trees and the next house, gray and plain. In front of the window was a desk. It had a small black metal lamp on it, a red mug holding a few pens and pencils, a new box of pencil crayons and a thick pad of paper. A small backpack sporting the logo of the local basketball team hung over the back of the chair. To the right of the desk stood a bedside table and then a bed. The bed had a blue spread on it, same color as the curtains. Chance's small suitcase and sports bag were sitting on top of the spread. Two posters were tacked onto the wall above the bed. One showed all the planets in orbit around the sun. The other showed the night sky, with the Big Dipper dead center. The bedside table had a clock radio and another black metal lamp.

A card was propped up against the lamp. He hadn't noticed it when Doug and Angie had shown him the room earlier. On the card was a picture of some men and boys fishing.

Chance walked across to the bed and

sat down. He put the cookies on the table and picked up the card. First he looked at the picture for a long time. It showed three men and two boys in a big rowboat. They were in the middle of a lake. Every one of them was sprawled in the boat, holding a fishing pole, some sort of hat pulled down over his eyes. Five fishing lines entered the still water. Mist rose gently into the bright sky. The cement in Chance's throat threatened to crack.

He opened the card. It was full of words. Happy words, he was sure. Welcoming words. He looked at the words for even longer than he had looked at the picture. Then he laid the card down flat, picked up the cookies and dropped them into the wastepaper basket beside the desk, lay down on the bed and turned his back to the room, the house, the crying baby and the kind and happy people.

Chapter Four

It felt to Chance as if hours passed while he lay there. The hands on the clock on the bedside table moved around and around, but round-faced clocks had never made sense to Chance. The baby's wailing and screaming started and stopped, started and stopped. Feet traveled up and down the stairs and along the hallway. Twice they paused outside his door. The second time a gentle voice called his name, but he waited and the voice stopped, the feet passed on.

The front door slammed soon after that. A boy's voice called, "I'm home." Then, "Is he here yet?" If any conversation followed, it was too quiet for Chance to hear.

He was just wondering whether he should peek out the door when it opened and someone stepped into his room. Chance felt the bed shift as Doug sat down.

"I have a feeling that you're awake," he said, putting his hand on Chance's ankle. Almost without knowing he was doing it, Chance kicked his hand off and scrambled to a sitting position at the head of the bed.

"Listen," Doug went on as if nothing had happened, "I know it's rough to come to a new house. But we want you to get off to a good start. The longer you hide out up here, the harder it will get. Now, up you get. Mark is downstairs and I want you to meet him."

Chance picked up a cushion and started twisting at the button in its center. He wasn't going down there to meet that boy. "Come on, Chance," Doug said. Chance looked up, met Doug's eyes for a moment, shook his head and turned his attention back to the cushion.

"All right. If you want to stay put, I can bring Mark up here to meet you. How about that?"

Well, you had to give the guy credit. He didn't give up, and he knew what was going on. Chance got off the bed and led the way out the bedroom door. But he waited at the top of the stairs for Doug to pass by.

Mark was watching TV in the den. Chance looked him over. His hair was cut close to his head. Supposed to be tough, Chance thought. Mark was pale and pretty skinny, but tall, the wiry type. Finally, he looked up, meeting Chance's eyes first and then looking him over. "Hi," he said, and turned back to the screen.

Chance opened his mouth to say hi back, but only a squeak came out, resulting in another glance and a small smile from the other boy. "Mark!" Doug's voice was sharp. "Turn that off, come over here and meet your new foster brother."

"I said hi," Mark said, but he clicked the remote, got up and came. Chance pushed his shoe against the edge of carpet in the doorway. There Mark stood, facing Chance. There Chance stood, facing the floor. He raised his chin and looked at Mark again. Mark looked back. Doug watched them for a moment and then relented.

"Come on, boys," he said. "That chicken is roasted to perfection!"

"Watch out for Louise," Angie said, looking up from the electric mixer as they walked into the kitchen. Chance looked around, then down. There was Louise on a quilt on the floor, surrounded by stuffed animals. On the counter sat the chicken, golden brown. The rest of the room was a madhouse: potato peelings, onion skins and dirty pots and pans covered every counter and filled the sink.

Mark got busy setting the table and Doug started carving the chicken. Chance moved into the room and sat down on a chair at the cluttered kitchen table. Angie smiled at him and winked. He looked away and then jumped as Louise gave a loud wail.

Angie turned off the beater. "Could you distract her for a minute?" she said. "I'll put her in her high chair as soon as I get these potatoes on the table."

Chance stared down at Louise. Her face was red, her eyes were squeezed shut, and her wide-open almost toothless mouth looked as if it was just getting geared up. Chance got down on his knees, clutched a stuffed rabbit and waved it over her. The screams continued. He dropped the rabbit, backed away and looked to see if Angie was coming, but she was spooning green peas into a bowl. Yuck, he thought, and turned back to Louise. Her hands were balled into fists by her chest. He reached down and wrapped his fingers around one of those fists. The screams stopped. Her eyes opened. For a long second they stared right into one another's eyes. Then she squeezed her eyes shut and let out the loudest yell yet.

"Thanks, Chance," Angie said, suddenly on her knees at his side. She reached under Louise, pulled a little blanket around her and swept her up into her arms. "I'm going to sit with Louise for a while in the other room. You go on in and get started.

Doug's dishing up." And she was gone.

Chance stood and looked toward the dining room door. He bit down hard on his lower lip. He looked toward the door to the front hall, toward the room from which Louise's wails, a little quieter now, were coming.

"Come and get it," Doug called. Chance wanted to go back to his room or to go into the front room and sit with Angie, wailing baby or no wailing baby. But he turned himself around, walked into the dining room and sat down in front of a plate heaped with food. Across the table, Mark was already gnawing on a drumstick. Chance picked up his knife and fork, even though he knew no food was going to get down his throat while he sat at this table.

Doug left him alone for a while. He asked Mark questions about his day, about school. "Didn't you have Ms. Samson in grade three?" he said at one point.

"Yeah. She was fantastic!" Mark said, his voice warm for the first time.

"She's going to be Chance's teacher,"

Doug said, meeting Chance's eyes for a moment. "Isn't that great?"

"I guess," Mark said, but the look he gave Chance showed that he did not think that it was great at all.

Doug turned his attention to Chance. "She does a lot of interesting things with her classes," he said. "I'm sure you'll like her. What's your favorite subject at school, anyway?"

Chance stared. A favorite subject? That was a joke. "I dunno," he said.

"Well, I think you'll develop some favorites here. It really is a wonderful school! You'll see for yourself tomorrow."

Chance's stomach turned upside down. School tomorrow? If he had eaten a bite, he'd be throwing it up right now.

"May I be excused?" he asked. "I don't feel so great."

"Don't you want dessert?" Doug said. Then he looked at Chance's plate. "Hey, you haven't eaten a bite."

"He's freaked out about school," Mark said. Chance thought he sounded pleased.

"Drop it, Mark," Doug said. "All right, Chance. Off you go. One of us will be up to check on you after dinner."

Chance sat on his bed and gripped the edge with his hands.

School.

He had never had to go to school on the first day. Never. And if foster houses were bad, schools were worse. In schools, they found out what you were worst at and made you do it over and over and over. In schools, the other kids always knew you were a foster kid. And they hated foster kids.

Chance grabbed the pencil crayons off his desk. He started with the purple pencil, sinking his teeth into it, deep into the wood, taking it out of his mouth and breaking it in two. Snap. He did the same to each piece. Snap. Snap.

His stomach rumbled. He leaned forward and looked in the wastepaper basket. There were the cookies under a heap of pencil fragments. He grabbed the top one, gave it a shake and ate it in huge, ravenous bites. Just as he was wiping the crumbs off his chest, Angie opened the door a crack. "I'll be in in a minute," she whispered, showing him Louise sleeping in her arms.

He stood up and looked in the mirror over the dresser on the other side of the room. He usually liked his gray eyes and heavy dark brows, but today his eyes looked small and red and his brown hair needed a comb. He smoothed it down as best he could with his hands.

His first day there was almost done.

Chapter Five

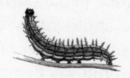

The second day was even worse. That was when he found out what dinners were really like there.

First came school. Ms. Samson seemed all right, but the other kids took a dislike to him like they always did and by the end of recess he'd seen the inside of the principal's office. When Angie and Louise picked him up at three o'clock, he was glad to get away, and equally glad that Mark was staying at school for a soccer practice.

But Mark had arrived by suppertime.

"Time to eat, boys," Angie called. Then,

"Chance, your supper's ready." A special invitation just for him.

When Chance entered the kitchen, Angie was already busy with Louise. She did look over and give him a smile, but she turned right back to what she was doing. He could hear the TV going in the other room, Mark's laugh at some show and the clink of cutlery. A plate had been prepared for Chance and waited on the kitchen table.

"I have to concentrate on this one," Angie said. "At least on weekdays supper's pretty casual around here. I'll take a look at your homework after Louise is asleep. You're welcome to sit here with me or to join Mark." She gestured with her chin toward the other room.

Chance picked up his plate and knife and fork and walked through the den door. There he stopped dead and waited for a clue. Mark was sitting at the far end of the couch. His plate was balanced on his knees, but he was caught up in what he was watching and noticing neither the food in his lap nor the boy in the doorway.

A few footsteps into the room, though, and Chance had Mark's attention. His eyes were chilly and blue and unblinking. "What do you want?" he asked.

"I, ah, do you mind if I eat here too?"

"Hey, eat where you want, kid. But if you're looking for a friendly eating companion, you came to the wrong place. I've gotta tell you something right off. If I wanted a brother, it would be a real one, not some stray. So just keep your distance. Got it?"

Chance stood and stared for long seconds after Mark had taken another bite and turned back to the TV. Then he walked out of the den by the other door, into the front hall and up the stairs to his bedroom. He let his plate clatter onto his desk and sat on the bed, jaw clenched. Yes, he got it.

The words, "A real one, not some stray," echoed through Chance's head as clear as if Mark was right there in his room taunting him. Finally, Chance got up, took his dinner plate, and tipped it into the wastepaper basket. The knife, fork and food landed in a heap on top of the pencil fragments and cookie crumbs. Then he picked up the card with the fishing men and boys. He looked at it, but the words blurred. Chance was pretty sure that the word "family" was on there, and he knew that was a lie. Bit by bit, he tore the card into tiny pieces, letting each shred of paper flutter into the basket on top of his dinner. When he was done, he dropped the plate on top of the whole mess, feeling only a slight twinge when it broke in two. Then he pulled back the covers on his bed, wrapped his arms around his pillow and curled up as small as he could.

When Doug came in later, Chance pretended to be asleep. Doug tucked the covers around his shoulders and whispered, "I don't know exactly what happened with Mark. I talked to him, but if you ever need to talk to me about trouble with him or with kids at school, I'm right here." It seemed like ages before Doug slipped out the door again.

In the morning, when Chance woke up, the wastepaper basket — plate, knife, fork and all — was gone. Well, Doug had acted nice, but what father was going to side with some stray against his own kid? Chance had learned long ago that you don't tell on the "real" kids.

From then on, whenever Mark was in the room something in Chance froze. He became still. Careful.

Once again, his greatest fear had been confirmed. Chance did not belong anywhere, with anyone. No matter how friendly Doug and Angie were, Mark's words drowned out their kindness:

"If I wanted a brother, it would be a real one. Not some stray."

Chapter Six

The caterpillars grew and grew. Every few days, the children took the little containers to their desks and examined the tiny creatures. Chance didn't always manage to get his caterpillar in the rush, but he stopped by the ledge at least once a day, picked out the container with the nick in the lid and checked for movement and growth.

One week after that first morning, on the same day that the new kid, Ken, showed up, Chance decided that he needed to get a real look at Matilda. That was what he had named her. Lunch was the best time. Ms. Samson always went to the staff room then, and after they had finished eating, no one was allowed to be inside. Chance was usually the last to leave, delaying the lunch monitors' departure and getting his name on the board for refusing to co-operate. Today when the outside bell rang, Chance went out right away, leaving the lunch monitors behind, mouths agape with shock. He went straight around to another door and re-entered the school. The next few minutes he spent in a cubicle in the upstairs washroom. Then he slipped out, down the stairs and into the classroom. Perfect. The room was empty.

He closed the door behind him, fetched Matilda off the ledge and a magnifying glass off the low shelf where they were kept. Then he settled down at his desk. He eased the lid off the container. There she was, fat, fuzzy and beautiful.

He tipped her out onto the desktop. She was many times the size she had been last week. Soon she would be ready to become a chrysalis. He gave her a little poke with his finger and she began to crawl, seeming to sense her way with her waving whiskers. Her body wiggled back and forth as she moved forward. He pulled the magnifying glass out of its box and held it up to his eye. Matilda doubled in size again. Chance was transfixed. The colours, the pattern, the delicate little hairs — she was gorgeous! He stared and stared, pushing her in a different direction whenever she came too close to the side of the desk. She felt soft and alive to his touch.

Then, with no warning, the bell rang. Lunch break was over. Chance leapt to his feet and stared wildly at the doors. Then he pulled himself together. He just had to put her back, that was all. It would take a while for Ms. Samson to let the kids in at the side door. He turned back to his desk and froze in shock. Matilda was gone!

The floor. Chance backed away and dropped to his knees. He must have brushed her to the ground when he jumped up. He started searching the floor beside his desk. He didn't find the caterpillar until he looked farther away, under his new neighbor's desk. He must have sent her flying. There she was, curled up on her side. Dead? Or hurt? She was still, not struggling to turn over, not moving at all. Something that looked like thin thread lay on the floor beside her. She had tried to save herself, like a spider, Chance thought. His eyes and the inside of his nose prickled. Within seconds, the door would burst open and twenty-five children with big stomping feet and mean hands would storm into the room. He made his fingers into gentle pincers, reached out and lifted Matilda off the carpet. Without getting up, he reached for the container on his desk. As children streamed into the room, he nestled Matilda into her cup and watched her for a moment. Yes, there was movement. She was alive. But he had no way of knowing how badly hurt she was.

He snapped the lid firmly into place and slipped the container into his desk. Matilda needed him now. He wasn't going to put her back in that crowd of caterpillars where any child in Division Seven could get his hands on her.

He would see to it that she was safe.

Chapter Seven

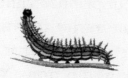

Once Matilda was in his desk, it was natural to bring her to the house. Chance passed casually by his desk on his way out the door that afternoon. His new neighbor, Ken, was still seated, copying something slowly, slowly, into his planner. Keeping one eye on Ken, Chance reached into his desk and closed his fingers tight around Matilda's cup. She wouldn't be safe in his pocket or his bag. So he carried her in his hand.

He had checked on her earlier, during silent reading. And had let out his breath in a whoosh of relief almost loud enough to turn Ms. Samson's eyes his way. Matilda was fine. Just like before.

"Would you move it?" Mark called from the doorway.

"All right, Mark. He's on his way," Ms. Samson said, looking up from her marking. "Do you have everything, Chance? Don't forget to get your planner signed." She smiled warmly at him as he left the classroom. Chance's eyes skipped from her to Ken, who was looking up now. Was Ken looking at Chance's hand? Had he seen?

The teacher's protection stopped at the classroom door. Mark bumped into Chance as he passed. "If I have to walk with you every day, kid, you better not make me wait." Chance held tight to his secret cargo and stayed quiet. Mark bumped him again, harder, once they were off the school grounds. "Did you hear me? I'm doing you a favor here, but not because I want to."

Chance's mouth was dry. His feet kept moving, but the rest of him didn't work, somehow. Angie and Doug had only started making Mark walk with him this week. Before that one of them had picked him up. Each day, Mark let him know how much he resented the task. On the weekend, Chance had overheard him yelling at his parents, "But why do we have to have them here? We were just fine the way we were. Anyway, I wanted a real brother, not somebody else's messed-up brat."

There was a pause, and Chance knew that Angie or Doug was replying in a calmer voice. Then Mark's shouts continued, growing tearful before they finally stopped altogether. The last words Chance heard him say were, "I didn't ask for them to come, so why should I have to help out? Why can't he walk by himself?"

On Monday, Chance had done just that. If Mark didn't want to walk with him, he could perfectly well walk by himself. After all, he was eight. Mark was only two years older.

Chance had been first out of the class, leaving behind homework, planner, everything but his coat. He had been outside almost before the bell stopped ringing. And he had run, determination and satisfaction coursing through him. Let Mark look and look for him. He had run like the wind, making at least one driver step on the brakes and the horn at the same time as he flew through a crosswalk. He had burst into the house, out of breath, but making up for it in exhilaration.

Angie came out into the hall holding Louise.

"Well, you're here awfully fast," Angie said, loudly enough to be heard over the sad baby's cries. Then, as she looked behind Chance at the closed door, "Where's Mark?"

"I don't know," Chance said.

"You came on your own?" Her voice was worried and maybe a little angry, but Chance didn't care. He just shrugged his shoulders.

"I can walk on my own," he said. "Other kids in my class do."

But Chance knew that wasn't strictly true, and so did Angie. They walked with friends or younger brothers or sisters. The school had a rule; no one under grade five was to walk to or from school alone. Even grade six kids were encouraged to walk with a buddy.

"Until you have someone else to walk with," Angie said, "you will walk with Mark, like it or not." She shifted Louise to her other arm, making soothing noises as she did so. Then she went on, "I know Mark is being rough on you, but he'll come around. You'll see."

"He hates me," Chance muttered.

"What did you say?" Angie asked, but instead of answering, Chance turned and ran up the stairs. Behind him the front door opened.

"There you are, you little creep," Mark called after him up the stairs.

Chance didn't turn his head, but he did listen with some satisfaction as Angie ordered Mark into the kitchen.

After Angie and Doug talked to him and Mark together that evening and made them both promise to stick together, Chance put up with Mark's reluctant company. It still hurt every time Mark bumped into him or whispered something mean into his ear, but he dulled the pain by making himself go hard inside. He just walked along, robot-like.

Today, Matilda clutched in his hand, he followed Mark. He stayed a few paces behind when he could, but no matter what, he said not a word and kept his eyes on the ground. He was so worried about Mark finding out what he had in his hand that his tongue was frozen anyway. He couldn't have spoken if he had wanted to, but he did like how mad Mark got when he ignored him.

Eventually, Mark decided to punish Chance with speed. "You'd better keep up," he shouted over his shoulder as he broke into a trot. Chance increased his pace, but kept a safe gap between himself and his assigned protector.

At least Mark had never glanced at Chance's closed fist or asked what he was carrying. So, as Chance huffed and puffed along, he turned over ideas about where Matilda was going. In his room, of course. He thought it would be good for her to have a bigger space than that puny plastic thing. And maybe some leaves, some real food. The video on Painted Ladies that the class had watched had said caterpillars liked leaves. In class, Ms. Samson had talked about making a chart of all the plants that Painted Lady caterpillars and butterflies liked to eat, but they hadn't done it yet. Never mind. He would give her some leaves and let her live like a caterpillar was really supposed to.

Well, sort of. A caterpillar wasn't really supposed to live in a house or a classroom or a little plastic container or a big comfy cage. A caterpillar was supposed to be free.

Chance thought about that for a moment. It had never occurred to him to let Matilda go. She belonged with him. Didn't she?

"Get a move on," Mark called over his shoulder. Chance looked up to find himself two houses behind. He ran to catch up. They were almost there anyway.

Mark left him at the driveway. He was off to hang out with his friends at the park. Chance walked into the house alone. The front hall was empty, so it was safe to set Matilda down on the cloak-stand shelf while he wriggled out of his coat. Actually, the house was surprisingly quiet. Louise must be sleeping, he thought. Leaving his coat and pack in a heap, he picked up Matilda and crept toward the stairs. Whatever Angie was doing, he wanted her to keep doing it.

Once upstairs, he saw that Louise's door was shut. He could hear the faint sound of the music Angie played to help her sleep. Angie and Doug's door was ajar. He peeked inside as he walked past. There was Angie, fast asleep on the bed. A little snorty sound made him jump, but it was just her version of a snore. Good; he could get to work without any interference.

After sitting on his bed, looking around the room and thinking a bit, Chance decided on Tupperware. It was mostly see-through and he could cover the top with plastic wrap. He'd punch little holes in it, so Matilda could breathe. And he'd collect some leaves from behind the house.

Chance tiptoed down the stairs and slipped out the back door. He grabbed a handful of leaves off the first plant he saw. A couple of small branches came away in his hand too. Oh well, it would have to do. A quick rummage through the big bottom drawer in the kitchen unearthed the perfect container, almost transparent, deep and wide and square. Tucking the roll of plastic wrap under his arm, clutching the Tupperware and a fistful of leaves, he took the stairs at a run.

"Chance, what's all that?" Angie was standing in her doorway, yawning and running her hands through her hair. The words were squeezed out through the yawn, but when she really took in what Chance was holding, she stepped forward. "Chance, what on earth are you up to? You've got half my rhododendron there!"

Chapter Eight

Chance looked down at his hands, at the leaves. Would she guess? The leaves were the big clue, he guessed. But if she figured it out, she would make him take the caterpillar back to school. She knew about the butterflies. It had been in the class newsletter last week. He would have to take Matilda back. He would lose her.

"Art," he blurted. Then he collected himself. "Yes, art. I'm going to make leaf prints. This is for the water." He held up the container. "This is to put down under the paper." He held up the roll of plastic. "And these are the leaves," he finished, falling silent and looking pleadingly at Angie.

"Newspaper would be better underneath," she said, though she was still looking at him oddly. "Do you need help getting set up? Did you borrow Mark's paints?"

Chance's stomach started to relax, but no, it was too soon for that.

"Here, let me help you. I'll get some newspaper from downstairs. Why don't you fill that with water from the bathroom? Wouldn't the kitchen table be ..."

Louise saved him. Maybe their voices woke her or maybe she was just ready to wail once more. A rising scream drowned out the music playing in Louise's room and drove any thought of Chance's painting from Angie's mind.

That was when Chance discovered that his bedroom door locked. He just hoped Angie didn't remember to ask to see a leaf picture. Safe in his room, he set both containers, the big empty one and Matilda's cup, on his bedside table. He picked the biggest, thickest, shiniest leaves and lined the bottom of the big container.

Then he opened the little one and watched Matilda for a moment. Most of the pasty food from school was gone. She turned from side to side and raised her head toward the window. He knew she couldn't see much, but he figured she noticed the brightness. He watched to see if she would move in that direction, and she did. She started to climb right over the edge of her little house.

Chance picked her up and put her in on top of the leaves. Maybe her new house would fit on the windowsill behind the curtain. He was just trying it there when his doorknob rattled.

"What's going on in there, Chance?" Angie called. "I don't want you locking your door. It's not safe."

Chance pulled the curtain across far enough to cover the box. "Coming," he called. "I didn't mean to lock it," he said as he opened the door. "I think it just locked on its own."

"What happened to the painting idea?" she asked, stepping into the room.

"I dunno," Chance said quickly. "Thought

I'd do my homework first and now I'm starving. Is it almost time to eat?"

Weeks ago he had learned that Angie liked feeding hungry kids. Now he put the knowledge to good use. The next half-hour was blissful: in the den, sitting on the carpet, eating graham crackers and peanut butter, watching an ancient rerun with Angie, some show called *Family Ties*, and entertaining Louise, who was happy for once, rolling around on her blanket.

Sure, Mark would be there soon and it would be over, but for now, Matilda snug upstairs and Louise, Angie and the television all to himself, Chance forgot that he was an unwanted foster child. Right now he was just a kid.

Chapter Nine

Matilda still seemed snug in her big new space when Chance left for school the next morning. But in the classroom he had a scare right off. A double-barreled scare, actually. First, Ms. Samson asked Martha to distribute the caterpillars. But, after she'd politely handed them out to everyone else, Martha found herself empty-handed.

"There's none left," she said, surprised.

"What do you mean?" Ms. Samson said. "There are twenty-six of you and twenty-six of them. Did you look carefully?"

"Yes," Martha said. "There isn't another one."

"Chance, do you have two at your desk?"

Ms. Samson asked bluntly. "Did you take an extra one?"

"No." Chance was angry. Guilty, but angry. "I have one here. One. Just like everybody else."

"All right, Chance. That's enough. Boys and girls, leave your caterpillars on your desks, right in the middle of your desks, and search."

So they searched. Chance searched hardest of all. He crawled under tables, rifled through the cloakroom and turned the art supply shelf inside out. Halfway through his search, he came face to face with Ken.

Ken stepped close. "You tell," he said.

"Tell what?" Chance said back, daring. This kid had hardly spoken a word in class yet. He didn't even speak English. But he was managing right now.

"You know," he said.

"No, I don't know," Chance replied, and shouldered past him to continue the search.

A good bit of cleaning up was required by the time they were done. But not a caterpillar did they find.

So Martha and another girl had to share a caterpillar that day. Everyone was worried about the lost caterpillar, but what else, Ms. Samson asked, could they do?

She got lots of answers to her question, a lot of theories about what had happened to the missing caterpillar and a lot of ideas about what to do about it. Chance did not contribute to the debate. He thought about Matilda, happy in her nice big box with all her green leaves. And he smiled inside himself. So what if everyone else was upset? He had saved Matilda. That was what mattered.

While he'd listened to the discussion, Chance had been peering through the sides of the plastic container on his desk. Now he stopped listening and stared intently. Something was different in there — wrong, maybe. The caterpillar wasn't moving right. She was dangling. Her bottom part was wriggling around, but her top end was stuck to the lid, right in the middle of the lid.

As the realization hit him, he was out of his desk and shouting all in a second. "Hey, she's turning into a chrysalis. She's attaching!" He danced around the room, holding the container high in the air.

Ms. Samson's hand came down firm on his wrist from behind. "Give her to me, Chance. Let me see," she said. And he did. All of a sudden frightened. What had his jumping done to the little creature? Had he hurt her?

But no, she was fine. And yes, she was getting ready to change form. The lost caterpillar was forgotten as everyone turned to see if his or her caterpillar was attaching too. And six were.

Ms. Samson explained that the caterpillars would start forming their chrysalides now. That would take about two days, she said. It would take two days for them to build their protection so they could turn into butterflies. When the chrysalides were ready, she would take the lids from which they hung and tape them to the butterfly bush, leaving the tiny creatures hanging freely.

Chance turned to look at the back of the room where the bush waited on a low table, planted in a big bucket and covered with netting. He couldn't wait to see the chrysalides hanging there.

At the same time, though, he wondered what he would find when he pulled back his curtain later that day. Matilda would want to attach like the others. Maybe she was trying to right this minute. But what did she have to attach herself to?

Chapter Ten

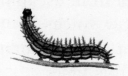

"Move it, kid," Mark called from the door-way, as he did every day.

And, "He'll be right with you, Mark," Ms. Samson said, as she did every day. But today, she didn't stop there. "Have you seen our butterfly bush? We have six chrysalides now!" she said. "It's hard to believe that it's already two years since you were helping me with the very first butterfly bush at our school."

"Yeah," Mark said. "It was amazing!" And he walked into the room and over to the bush. Chance watched in horror from the cloakroom. That bush had nothing to do with Mark. It was not Mark's business. And now it was turning out that Mark had done it already. Two years ago.

"I'm ready," Chance said, stepping forward. But both foster brother and teacher ignored him. They were standing together, gazing through the netting that would keep the butterflies from escaping, and talking together in low voices.

"I said, I'm ready," Chance said again, more loudly this time.

"Yeah, all right, Chance. Give me a break, okay?"

It was not okay, and it got worse. "We seem to have lost one," Ms. Samson was saying.

"That's awful!" Mark responded. "Remember when that happened to us? We were so sad." Chance almost forgot his horror that Ms. Samson was telling Mark about the lost caterpillar in his shock that Mark could talk like that.

"No, no, none have died. At least I hope not! One disappeared," Ms. Samson said.

That was it. This conversation had gone way further than it should have. Chance gathered himself together and spoke more words to his foster brother than ever before.

"We have to go right now, Mark. Angie said. We're all going out somewhere or something. Remember? She said to set off right away after school." Chance reached out and pulled on Mark's sleeve while he spoke. Mark flicked his hand away in disgust. But he also stared at Chance in surprise at the insistence and at all those words.

"All right, off you go, boys," Ms. Samson said. "Come back any time, Mark."

Chance hoped Mark had missed that last bit.

As they were walking together that day Mark seemed to forget that Chance was beneath contempt. Or maybe he just forgot who Chance was altogether. He talked on and on at him about being in Ms. Samson's class and about raising butterflies.

He was stealing the whole thing, doing it first, knowing everything already. At least he didn't know about Matilda. Or so Chance thought.

"So, one of the caterpillars is missing.

I'd be willing to bet you know something about that, kid," Mark said.

For the first time in Mark's company, Chance was too angry to be scared. "Yeah, so one's missing. What's that got to do with you?" he said, glaring up at Mark.

Surprise and sudden anger stopped Mark in his tracks. He looked around. They were walking by the overgrown vacant lot. No one was in sight. Without warning, he grabbed Chance by the shoulders and spoke again, this time in his slowest, meanest voice. With each sentence, his fingers dug deeper.

"I'll say it has something to do with me. If you've done something to mess up Ms. Samson's butterflies, that has a whole lot to do with me. And I can tell you that my mum and dad wouldn't want a kid in the house who would do something to mess up a class project."

With no warning, Chance head-butted him. Rage drove the top of his head right into Mark's chest. Hard. Mark grunted and let go. Chance ran. He had only a block to go; looking back when he turned up

the walk, he could see Mark still standing in the same spot. He flung himself into the house, ignored Angie's "hello" from the living room, took the stairs three at a time and shut his bedroom door behind him with a gasp of relief.

He pulled back the curtain and grabbed the box off the sill. No, Matilda was not attaching. She was curled up half under a leaf in the corner. She looked awfully still. He gave her a poke. But no, she was all right. She moved under his finger. Just sleeping, he guessed.

But a seed of worry planted itself in his mind.

He put the box on his bedside table where he could watch it and sat down on the bed, rubbing his head. It was sore where he had bashed it into Mark's bony chest. Thinking of the impact, he grinned in satisfaction. That would teach Mark to leave him and his caterpillar alone.

Then he thought of what Mark had said. That Angie and Doug wouldn't want him if they knew what he had done. No. Angie and Doug were keeper foster parents. If you were a baby, you could cry and cry. If you were older, eight years old, for example, you could break things. You could get three out of twenty on a spelling test. And you could keep a stolen caterpillar in your room. Angie and Doug didn't send kids back. For a moment Chance wondered why he wanted to stay in this house anyway, with a screaming baby and a boy who hated him. Who could say? But he did.

A sharp knock on the door interrupted his thoughts. He leapt to his feet and was standing with Matilda's box thrust behind him when the door opened. Doug stood there. Mark was hovering behind him.

"I'd like to see you downstairs, please. In the kitchen," Doug said. The words were stern, but his eyes were warm. Chance was pretty sure that Doug knew that he wouldn't head-butt Mark without some sort of a reason. Still, his heart pounded. He stood, hands hidden behind his back, and waited for Doug and Mark to turn and go.

But, "Hey, ask him what he's got behind

his back!" Mark said. "Come on, Dad. It's that caterpillar. I'm telling you."

But Doug would not be drawn in. "Chance is meeting us in the kitchen," he said to his son. "You go ahead."

So Mark was forced to lead the way. And Chance was able to put Matilda back behind the curtain before making his own way slowly downstairs.

Chapter Eleven

Mark was so angry that Doug got annoyed and sent him away. "Yes, I have seen the red mark on your chest, son," he said. "I agree that there's no excuse for that, but I still want to hear Chance's side of the story. Off you go, so Chance and I can talk together quietly."

Mark stamped his way out of the kitchen, but he didn't say a word in argument. Chance should have sensed danger. But he was worrying instead. Worrying about being sent away. These are keeper foster parents, he repeated to himself. Still, keeper or no, a foster parent was not the same as a real parent.

Chance kicked at his chair leg and kept his eyes on the table. It was that hard plastic stuff and it had lots of interesting cracks, stains and scratches. Doug talked on and on in his gentle voice, and the words floated away, up, up and away. Like balloons, Chance thought.

Finally, Doug reached out and gripped Chance's shoulder.

Like son, like father, Chance thought, but he stopped kicking.

"Look at me," Doug said, sharply now. Chance looked, but gave another kick at the same time.

"We do not accept violence in this house," Doug said. "Neither you nor Mark is permitted to hurt the other in any way. Is that understood?"

In answer, Chance wiggled his shoulder, still in Doug's grip. He wasn't holding on hard, but it hurt because of Mark's earlier attack.

Doug let go. Chance nodded his head once.

"All right. If you refuse to tell me your

side of the story, you'd best be off."

And Chance was off, in an instant. Out the door, into the hall and up the stairs. As he neared the top, fear entered his heart. He could hear music from Mark's room. His door was closed. Chance headed for his own room, but he already knew what he would find.

His own door, carefully shut behind him when he went downstairs, stood open. From the doorway he could see that the curtain had been pulled back.

The windowsill was bare.

Matilda was gone.

Chapter Twelve

At least Mark's door wasn't locked. Chance opened it as quietly as he could.

Mark was sitting at his desk, hunched over something. Chance didn't have to see it to know what it was.

"Give her back," he hissed. He did not want Doug to come upstairs to investigate.

Mark looked up. "It's dying," he said.

"Matilda's not an it. She's a she. And what do you mean? What have you done to her?"

"It. She. Doesn't make much difference now. You starved her to death, Chance," Mark said.

"No, I didn't. I gave her leaves, real leaves. Way better than that goop at school."

"But that goop is made out of stuff that caterpillars like. I don't know what these ones are, but anyone with any brains could see that they're too thick and hard for a caterpillar to eat. Anyway, she's not eating them."

Chance had walked close enough to see Matilda where she was curled up now, in Mark's palm. He didn't try to take her back. He just stood.

He had thought that he had known everything about Painted Ladies. Everything. Except for the one thing he needed to know to keep Matilda alive, to let her become a butterfly. She was lying there starving and it was his fault.

"She can't die, Mark, she can't. There must be some kind of leaves she likes. You have to help me."

"It's a little late for that," Mark said, chewing on the side of his thumb as he spoke. Then he was quiet for a long time.

Chance burst into the silence, "I'm taking

her back to school tomorrow. But there must be some leaves around here that she'll eat. Come on, let's go find all the kinds of leaves we can!"

"Not so fast, kid. You've done your bit, stealing her, starving her. I'm going to take her back to school tomorrow myself. If she survives the night."

If Chance could have grabbed Matilda out of Mark's hand right then, he would have, but Mark's fingers were curled around her. Anything that Chance did might hurt Matilda more than it would hurt Mark. Every single thing that he felt like doing would only make things worse.

So he tried something that he didn't feel like doing at all.

"Please, Mark," he said, hating how raw the words sounded in the room. "Please don't take her away from me."

"I have to," Mark said. "Ms. Samson would want me to."

And then Chance knew what to say, because he knew that wasn't true. "No, she wouldn't. She would want you to help me.

She would want us to work together. And she would want us to bring Matilda back to school first thing tomorrow morning."

"Well, you're right about the last thing, anyway," Mark said, seeming to relent. "All right, you can help me get food for her anyway. Then we'll see."

"What do you mean, 'we'll see'? She's my caterpillar. You can't do that."

"Watch me," said Mark. "You follow my rules, or get out of here right now."

Chance knew that he didn't have much choice. "Fine," he said. "What are we going to do?"

"We're going to go find thistles," Mark said. "I remember Ms. Samson said they like thistles and lots of other plants I can't remember, but I remember the thistles. I thought it was weird. So prickly. But that's what she said."

"I bet there're some in the vacant lot," Chance said. And they were off.

The thistles were there. But they were small and green in May; it took Chance and Mark a long time to decide they were thistles at all. Finally they agreed to let Matilda be the judge.

Doug was in the front hall holding Louise when the two of them burst through the front door. He stood and stared, speaking not a word, as the two enemies ran up the stairs full tilt, hands full of greenery. Even Louise seemed to realize that she was witnessing something out of the ordinary. She was as silent as Doug.

This time Chance held Matilda, along with several soft, downy leaves, while Mark emptied the old leaves into the garbage and filled the container with the rest of the fresh ones. The little caterpillar lay curled in Chance's palm, taking no notice of the food so close by. Chance picked her up and placed her right on a leaf and then lowered it into the container along with the others.

"Let's just leave her alone now," he said. "Maybe if we're not around she'll eat."

"Yeah," Mark said. "I'm keeping her here, though, in my room. We'll take her back to school together tomorrow morning like you said."

Chance stood for a moment, looking at Mark, seeing his determination. Then he looked at the container, Matilda invisible inside among the leaves, maybe eating, maybe not.

Well, Mark had to sleep sometime.

"All right," Chance said, and marched out of the room.

Back in his own room, he flung himself on his bed. As he rolled onto his back he saw that Mark had followed him and was standing in his doorway.

"Maybe now you understand why you shouldn't have taken the caterpillar, Chance," he was saying, his words tight. Chance's head throbbed. Whatever Doug might say, Mark had deserved that head in the chest.

"Get out," Chance said, sliding off the bed. "We're taking her back tomorrow, like you said. And she's in your room right now. So just get out."

"She'll probably be dead by then," Mark said. But he left.

Chapter Thirteen

Chance slammed his door and spun around, fists clenched. No more did Mark make him freeze up inside. Now he made him mad. Pretending to help and then taking the first chance to attack. Trying to teach him a lesson. And saying she would die! She wasn't going to die. She was probably munching away already. But Chance did not go back to Mark's room to check.

He didn't go down for supper either. Just ignored their calls. Maybe they would send him back. And maybe that would be best anyway.

Angie brought him his dinner.

She knocked, walked in and put a tray on his desk. "I don't like a member of the family refusing to come to the table, but I won't have you going hungry either," she said, her words as brisk as her knock. Then her voice softened. "I know Mark's hard on you and that it's the last thing you need to cope with." She pulled out the desk chair, took a seat and went on, "But he'll come around. He doesn't understand why we weren't happy with him, why he wasn't enough for us. It's funny. It's precisely because we love him so much that we wanted more children to love."

Chance stared at her in astonishment, but she just smiled and went on, "Because we love Mark so much, we wanted to bring you and Louise into our home so we could love you too." And with that she stood, pushed in the chair, touched Chance briefly on the top of his head and left the room.

Chance was not sure that what she said made a particle of sense. But it certainly gave him lots to think about.

He left the food. How could he eat, when that tiny creature was wasting away because of him? He did sleep, though, finally.

When he woke up, it was very late. The whole house had settled down, wrapped in flannel pajamas and nightgowns and sleepers. Chance was curled up on his bed, still in his jeans and T-shirt. The quilt had been tucked around him and his dinner tray was gone.

He curled up tighter, hugging himself. They could tuck him in, bring him dinner and tell him their nice little theories all they wanted. None of it made any difference where Mark was concerned.

Then he remembered Matilda.

His own loneliness forgotten, Chance crept from his bed and out into the hall. Mark's doorknob turned silently; his skin crackling with fear and anticipation, Chance stepped inside.

Luckily, the curtain wasn't closed properly. Light from a street lamp fell across the floor. Mark was a softly breathing hump under the blankets, but his desk, where Matilda had been earlier, was bare. Chance took a slow, shallow breath and looked around, but it was not until he had tiptoed right to Mark's bedside that he saw the Tupperware container pushed against the wall on Mark's bedside table. He managed to reach the container without making a sound, but as he pulled it back, his elbow caught on the bendy neck of the lamp. He froze. The hump on the bed shifted; the breathing sounds changed.

No longer trying to be quiet, Chance took Matilda and fled, out into the brightly-lit hall and back into his own dim room. He sat for a long moment on the side of his bed, catching his breath, waiting for his heart to settle back into his chest. Finally, he reached out and flipped on his light.

Then, about to pull back the plastic wrap, he paused. What if Mark was right? They might have been too late with the plants and she might be dead. Curled up and dead.

Steeling himself, he peered into the container. First off, he saw that she wasn't where she had been. One way or another, she had moved. He pulled the cellophane off the top and reached in, moving leaves aside with care. There she was in the bottom. Had she fallen there? Was she dead after all? But she wasn't on the plastic bottom. She was on a plant. As he watched, she inched her way forward and munched. He saw her munch on the plant. Then her head raised up, curious, and waved toward the light.

Chance's face split open in jubilation. He almost cheered out loud, but he stopped himself just in time. He did not want all those flannel figures rising from their beds. But he did have something to say to one. Dancing on quiet feet, he was outside Mark's room in a moment. Once again, he slipped inside.

"Mark," he hissed. "Mark, wake up."

Mark sat up, hair on end, eyes full of gluey sleep and squeezed tight against the light from the hall.

"Hey, it's the middle of the night! Get out of here."

"No, you gotta come and see," Chance said. "Come on."

But Mark just mumbled "Get out!" again, flopped down and turned his back.

Chance reached out to yank his blankets off, but then he had a better idea. Seconds later he was back at Mark's side.

"Mark," he hissed again. "Look!"

Mark rose up ready to fight, but between him and his target was a Tupperware container, held right under his nose. With his free hand, Chance flipped on the bedside light. Mark put his hands over his eyes and groaned.

"I told you she was going to die," he said. "You killed her. I told you."

Then he came fully awake. "And what are you doing with her anyway?"

"Just look," Chance said.

So Mark took the container into his hands and looked. It took him a moment to find Matilda, but when he did Chance watched his face light up just as Chance's had.

"Hey," Mark said. "She likes thistles, huh?"

"Yeah," Chance replied. "She likes thistles."

For a long moment Mark looked at Chance. Chance worked hard to hold his gaze. Finally, something changed in Mark's eyes.

"All right, kid. I gotta get some sleep. You want to keep her for the night, be my guest, but we're gonna take her back to school together in the morning."

"Sure," Chance said, and not wanting to risk another change of heart, he hastily left the room.

Chapter Fourteen

There was no way to hide the fact that the missing caterpillar had returned. Chance had put her back in the tiny plastic container on top of the leftover crumbs of food. He added a few shreds of thistle plant for good measure and held the container tight in his fist inside his pocket.

Mark had insisted on carrying it the whole way to school, to keep Matilda safe, he said, making anger bubble up in Chance once again. But they had arrived before the bell and Mark had been unable to resist the soccer field, so "Here you go, kid," he had said, and off he had gone.

Chance had the school door open before the bell had finished ringing, but other kids were close behind, some with parents in tow. They were all excited about the butterflies now too. Parents crowded into the classroom with their children to see the chrysalides slowly transforming inside their thin skins.

Once inside, Chance walked straight to the ledge where the slow bloomers were. He had Matilda out of his pocket now. He didn't have much time. Once they had seen the chrysalides, the kids always came en masse to see if any more caterpillars had attached. With his back to the butterfly bush, Chance whisked the lid off Matilda's tiny cup. Luckily, he had kept it, and it still had some goop inside, along with all the weird thready bits that the caterpillars left behind as they moved around. He grabbed the bits of thistle between his fingers and shoved them in his pocket.

"Time to attach, Matilda," he breathed as he snapped the lid back on and set her down on the shelf. Then he turned and headed casually to the cloakroom.

The cry he had been expecting came almost immediately. "Ms. Samson, Ms. Samson, there're eight now. The missing caterpillar is back! It's back!"

Chance finished getting his stuff out of his pack. He walked over to the bush and took a look at the chrysalides. Please let Matilda be one of them soon, he thought, ignoring the excited hubbub around the return of the missing caterpillar. He pulled a chair off the stack at the back of the room and headed for his desk. That was when his eyes met Ms. Samson's. She knows, he thought, looking right back at her without blinking. Well, what's she going to do about it?

"Good morning, Chance," she said. "Did you hear that our missing caterpillar has returned?"

"Yeah, that's great," Chance said as he settled down at his desk and waited for what she would do next.

That was when his eyes met Ken's. Chance couldn't decide which was stronger in Ken's expression, anger or curiosity.

Ms. Samson didn't give him time to find out. The class was to study their spelling words, she said, with small chalkboards and partners while Ms. Samson herself took the two caterpillars who had recently attached and whose chrysalides were now fully formed and found them their spots on the butterfly bush.

Two days later, one of the remaining caterpillars died. The whole class trooped outside in the rain to bury the tiny creature. Three children cried. Chance did not. But his stomach knotted up at the idea that tomorrow they might be burying Matilda. Or the day after that. And if they did, it would be his fault.

"Crybabies," he hissed as the class trooped back into the classroom.

"Ms. Samson," Ralph called instantly, infuriatingly.

"Tattle-tale," Chance said, at full volume now.

"Take your seat, Chance," Ms. Samson said. "I'll speak to you after school."

* * *

Mark had to wait outside the closed class-room door.

"What did you do now?" he asked when Chance was released.

"I didn't do anything. Leave me alone!" Chance took off at a run. Mark kept up, and when they burst through the door together he was good and mad. They both stopped in the front hall to fling off their coats and catch their breath. "I've been way nicer than you deserve, kid. I helped you save your little stolen pet's life. I let you wake me up in the middle of the night and shove a bunch of leaves in my face. And right this minute I couldn't tell you why I bother."

"You're not so nice," Chance said, but by the time he said it, he was halfway up the stairs.

Chapter Fifteen

Chance sank his teeth deep into his last pencil. It felt good, chewy with a slight crispness to the paint. He worked his way down from the eraser end, examining the perfect tooth marks after each chew.

Ten bites, evenly spaced, and on the tenth, snap. That was the formula. On the tenth bite, he gripped the tip of the pencil between his fingers, sank his teeth a little deeper and drove his chin down toward his chest hard. The pencil snapped.

Satisfied for the moment, he tossed the halves into his desk, where they joined the jumbled, crumpled mess that had gathered since his arrival in Ms. Samson's class. The math paper he was supposed to be working on would soon be added to the mix.

It was a page of word problems. Butterfly word problems, but butterflies were no different from dandelions or teacups where math was concerned. Actually, math, reading and writing combined. That's what word problems were.

Pencil disposed of, Chance looked around the room. Ken sat next to him.

He was carefully coloring in the butterflies on his page with pencil crayons. Ken's page was different from Chance's. Ken had a baby page. At least, that's what Martha and some of the other kids, the Martha clones, called it. All pictures and numbers, no words.

It seemed as if Ken didn't care when they said that, because he didn't understand English. He was even newer to the class than Chance was. And he had moved a lot farther to come here. All the way from Hong Kong across the Pacific Ocean, Ms. Samson said. Ken didn't seem to care when the other kids told substitute teachers about him either. "He can't do that," they would say, all serious, helping the teacher. "He doesn't understand English."

Chance cared, though. It made him mad, especially because half the time they were wrong anyway. And Chance suspected that when Ken sat there with his face all blank while they talked about him, he actually did understand. And if he did understand, then he cared too.

Chance cared even more when they said stuff about him. "He's always bad like that," they would say loudly. "You have to put his name on the board." Or, "You should keep him after school." Or, "Send him to the principal." As bossy as that, ordering around him and the substitute both.

He glanced at his paper again, but the words had done nothing to untangle themselves. He knew that if he tried he would probably be able to find the word "butterfly" in every problem. And there'd be number words. He knew those. But there were other words too. And with Matilda sitting on that ledge, all alone like she was, he just wasn't going to try.

Right now, this very minute, Ms. Samson was attaching the last three chrysalides to the butterfly bush. The last three, that is, except for Matilda. Matilda was still a caterpillar. A munching, crunching caterpillar. A caterpillar who could not get enough green guck to eat. But caterpillar through and through.

And Chance knew perfectly well that that was his fault.

Every bit on purpose, he crumpled up his paper, his butterfly-word-problem paper, and threw it right onto Ken's desk. Ken looked up, startled. And Chance grinned at him. He thought it was a friendly grin, like he was saying, "Forget the baby pages. Look at me!" And Ken *had* stopped coloring. He *was* looking at Chance. But he wasn't grinning back. Instead, he looked kind of mad.

And one of the Martha clones was calling out, "Ms. Samson, Chance is being bad again."

"Julie, unless you are in physical danger,

I do not appreciate tattling," Ms. Samson said from the butterfly bush.

"But Ms. Samson," said another of the clones, "he's bugging Ken. And Ken doesn't even know English."

"All right, Preeti," Ms. Samson said. Her voice was sharp. But she did look over. She took in Ken's angry face and the crumpled paper. The whole class watched, breathless, hoping, Chance knew, that she would *do* something. But Chance cut her off at the pass. He jumped up and grabbed the paper off Ken's desk, knocking Ken's pencil to the floor while he was at it.

"Pick up Ken's pencil," Ms. Samson said patiently. But not really. She wasn't patient at all.

Chance knew how to prove that. He could prove that Ms. Samson wasn't patient every time. He did it by moving slowly.

He headed for the recycling box.

"I said, pick up Ken's pencil, Chance," Ms. Samson said, her voice a little tighter now.

Chance tugged at the ball of paper until he found an edge. Then he smoothed it out. After all, they weren't supposed to put crumpled paper in the recycling box.

Now she was striding in his direction. And her shoes made sharp noises, even on the carpet. She walked right up to Chance, towered over him. Chance looked up at her. He paused. Then, just as she was taking in a good, big breath to speak to him again, he strode as smartly as she had over to Ken's desk, bent, picked up the pencil and handed it to Ken. He even tried a little smile, but Ken took the pencil from his hand without looking at him and without twitching a single muscle in his face.

Chance sat down and scuffed at the floor with his foot. So now Ms. Samson was mad at him, Ken was mad at him, and Matilda was going to be a caterpillar forever. She was probably going to die a caterpillar. And she had turned out to be such a greedy little caterpillar. She was always hungry.

That thought gave him the idea, the brilliant, best-ever idea.

Chapter Sixteen

Forgetting that he was in disgrace, he was at Ms. Samson's desk in a moment, whispering eagerly in her ear. And the more she listened, the more she smiled. When he finished, she nodded her head, turned and pulled a book off the rack by her desk.

She took the book and walked to the front of the class.

"I think that someone in this class would very much like to hear this story," she said, smiling.

"But we've all heard it a million times!" said Ralph, who always complained about rereading books, but then loved them as much as anyone else.

"Well, Ralph, maybe not a million times," Ms. Samson replied. "But there is someone in this class who I'm almost certain has *never* read *The Very Hungry Caterpillar*."

Martha's hand shot up. "It's Ken," she said when Ms. Samson gave her a chance. "You mean Ken."

"No, Ken was here when I read it a few weeks ago. No," she said, "put your hands down. We have one caterpillar left in this class. And she is a ..."

"Very hungry caterpillar," Chance filled in, joy flooding his heart. "Can I bring her to the story corner?"

"Yes, please do. And let's the rest of us get ready to tell our very last, very hungry caterpillar her very first story."

Ms. Samson let Chance hold the little creature in his palm so she could see the pictures. "Listen carefully, Matilda," he whispered to her. He held her a little closer to the book when the very hungry caterpillar turned himself into a cocoon — well, a chrysalis really, but they called it a cocoon in the book. Chance knew, as did the rest of the class, that if it were really a cocoon that would make her a moth instead of a butterfly.

Matilda lifted the front of her body right up, high in the air, and Ms. Samson looked over at her and smiled.

After the story was done, Chance took Matilda for a tour of the butterfly bush. "Look," he whispered to her. "One of those should be you. Soon you'll be a chrysalis too."

He looked down at her, nestled in his hand. That was when he noticed the chrysalis lying on the table under the bush. He scanned the bush, but couldn't find the lid that it had fallen from. It looked different from the other chrysalides, even the newest ones. He couldn't see the butterfly inside, just hard, whitish skin.

"Chance, it's time to get back to work," Ms. Samson said. "We're going to start making butterfly storyboards." And she held a big sheet of paper up to the class. It was divided into sixteen roomy squares. "With just pictures, just words or both, I want you to plan a story with a butterfly or a caterpillar in it," she said.

Chance looked down at the still, hard chrysalis for one more moment. Then he turned away, put Matilda back in her container on the ledge and settled down to work. The story was halfway unfolded in his mind before he had unearthed his pencil crayons from his desk.

Chapter Seventeen

Most of the class was eager to get out the door when the three o'clock bell rang. It was easy for Chance to linger unnoticed, putting the finishing touches to one of the squares on his storyboard, while he waited to have the classroom to himself. When he saw Mark hovering in the doorway, he beckoned him in.

Ms. Samson had been saying goodbye at the door, but now she was at her desk, reading over the storyboards. She had just said, "Time to go, Chance," as she passed his desk. Now she seemed to have forgotten that he was there, although Chance considered that unlikely.

Mark stood just inside the door, looking annoyed. "Come on, kid," he said. "Get it together. I don't have time for this."

Ms. Samson paused in her work. "Oh, hello, Mark. We read a book you'll remember. Your brother picked it out!" And she held up the book with the big green caterpillar on the cover. Mark came a few steps further into the room.

"Hey, I love that book!" he said. "But it's not a Painted Lady, is it? The very hungry caterpillar turns into a different kind of butterfly."

"That's right," Ms. Samson said. Mark was standing by her desk now, flipping through the book.

Chance stood up. "I want to show you something," he said in a loud, clear voice addressed to both his teacher and his foster brother. "But I think it's something bad," he added, and walked over to the butterfly bush without waiting for a reply.

Mark followed, but Ms. Samson stayed where she was.

"Oh, Chance," she said, "I was hoping no one would notice. I was going to take it away tonight."

"What?" Mark said. "What is it?"

And Chance pointed to the small gray object on the table under the bush. Then, without even asking if it was all right, he reached under the netting and took the little chrysalis into his hand. That was when he really knew that it was dead.

"We have to bury it," he said softly. "Near the caterpillar. We have to do it now. The other kids will freak out if they see this."

"Yes, Chance. Let's bury it. Mark, will you join us?"

And the three of them walked outside and buried the small dead creature. Chance felt sad, and he felt scared. Matilda had to live; she just had to!

On the walk to the house, Chance and Mark were quiet. But when Chance's hand was on the doorknob, Mark stopped him.

"That wasn't our caterpillar, was it?"

"No," Chance said quietly. "Our caterpillar is still a caterpillar. She eats and eats, but she won't attach. She just won't! That's why we read the book today. We read it to her, to teach her what she's supposed to do."

"Did she listen carefully?" Mark asked, smiling.

"I think she did," Chance answered. And he smiled back.

* * *

The next morning he flew to school, Mark on his heels.

"You can't get in anyway," Mark called out breathlessly, but Chance kept right on running.

Lots of kids were milling around at the entrance, under the overhang to keep out of the rain. Ralph was already stationed right by the door, and he wasn't about to give Chance his place.

"I was here first," he said in a strong, clear voice. "And you can keep your elbows to yourself."

Chance scowled, but he let Ralph have his way. A teacher was standing nearby, anyway. So he waited beside Ralph, right up against the door, ready to push his way in the second the bell went. The wait seemed extra long this morning.

When he finally did get into the room, rushed to the ledge and held the container up to the light, he wished that he had just stayed out there. Matilda was still a caterpillar.

That was the day the butterflies started coming out. Four, before recess.

Outside, at recess, in a fine drizzle, Chance went looking for Ralph. When he found him, he said loudly, "I'll keep my elbows to myself if you want, but say hello to my fist." And he punched him right in the gut. Ralph doubled over, but his friend turned to find the supervisor. She was right there. She had seen the whole thing. Chance spent the rest of recess in a chair outside the principal's office and the half-hour after recess in the principal's office, being talked at, talked at, talked at.

Why had he punched Ralph? she wanted to know. What kind of question was that?

Because Ralph was a know-it-all, bossy tattletale and he deserved it. Because every caterpillar but Chance's was turning into a butterfly and someone was going to pay. But those answers wouldn't satisfy Mrs. Laurence. They didn't even satisfy Chance. So Mrs. Laurence waited for an explanation that never came.

Finally, she gave up and phoned Angie. Ralph was called in and Chance had to apologize. The principal explained that she could suspend him right now, but that she was going to give him one more chance.

Then she got a grade six girl to walk him back to class.

"Hey, Chance, you missed it. Two more butterflies are out since recess," Martha informed him as soon as he was through the door.

So, on the way to his desk, Chance casually slid Martha's storyboard away from her, tore it in half and handed it back.

The grade six girl was still there. Ms. Samson had her walk Chance right back up to the office. Doug had to be called away from work to come get him, because Louise was napping and Angie couldn't get away. While he was waiting, the principal asked if anything was wrong at his house. Chance shook his head hard.

"All right," she said. "Let's see. It's Wednesday today. I don't like you missing school, Chance, but I can't have you here if you are going to punch other children or destroy their belongings. I think a two-day suspension will give you enough time to think about things. Plus the rest of today. So you'll be permitted back in the school on Monday, but the consequences will be much more serious if anything like this happens again. Is that understood?"

Her words washed over him at first, but all of a sudden what she was saying came through. She was suspending him until Monday. He couldn't stay away until Monday. Who knew what might happen between now and then?

"Mrs. Laurence, please," he said quickly. "I'll think about it all afternoon. I know I shouldn't have done that stuff. I know that.

I'll apologize to Ralph again. And to Martha. I'll tape her paper back together. But please let me come back to school tomorrow."

Mrs. Laurence looked surprised, but Chance figured that it was hard for a school principal to resist a kid who begged to come to school. And he figured right. When Doug arrived and took him away, not a word was said about Thursday and Friday. He was only being suspended for the day.

It was a quiet afternoon. Louise wasn't screaming quite so much lately. Chance spent a long time in the family room coaxing her to roll over and dangling a variety of toys within reach. Angie sat on the couch with a novel, turning a page once in a while, but slipping into a doze in between times.

At one point she said gently, "What's making you feel like punching kids, Chance, and tearing up their work? Is something wrong at school? Or here? Or is it stuff you're thinking about from before?"

Chance tucked his finger into Louise's palm and felt that satisfying, tight, baby grip. Angie's questions made him feel kind of good, even though he didn't have the answers to them either.

"I don't know," he mumbled back. "I just get mad sometimes."

"What happened that made you mad?" she asked.

"Nothing special," he said. He knew that he was mad about the butterflies and mad at himself, but how was he supposed to explain that?

Angie waited a moment and then turned back to her book. Chance put his hands around the baby's thick middle, picked her up and set her on his lap. She gurgled a grin at him and his stomach turned over in delight.

The afternoon wore on.

Chance was in his own little reverie, feeding Louise watered-down juice from a bottle, when Angie jumped up.

"Goodness," she said. "It's five to three and I've done nothing all afternoon!" She leaned down and took Louise from his arms. "I'm going to put her in her chair and get some laundry in."

Chance didn't like letting Louise go; he hated Angie's bustle and determination. The peaceful afternoon was over. But, come to think of it, maybe the timing was just right.

"I'll be out back," Chance called to Angie down the basement stairs. "See you, Louise," he said. Then, "See you, Sis," he tried. Not bad.

He went out the door that led from the kitchen into the backyard, but he didn't linger. He had about three minutes to get to school before the bell. At least six butterflies were fluttering around the butterfly bush and he hadn't even glanced their way in the morning. Now he was desperate to see them. To see them and to visit Matilda, the butterfly to be. He might get into more trouble or he might not. But as he ran the three blocks to school, he was the happiest he had been in a long time. Maybe ever, he thought, and discovered that it was hard to grin and gasp for breath at the same time.

He didn't quite make it. The bell went when he was still half a block away from school. But that should be okay, as long as Mark had been told that he was gone and didn't show up to get him, or didn't just come out first and see him. Mark's classroom was a long way away from the exit. He should be safe. And he was. He had mixed himself in with a crowd of grade fours and was well out of Mark's path when Mark left the school with a friend. Chance waited until Mark was across the street and well on his way before he slipped into the school and through the door to his own classroom.

"Hi, Ms. Samson," he said, startling her. "I'm sorry I tore Martha's storyboard. I could fix it for her if you like. But can I see the butterflies?" He spoke quickly, heading for the bush at the same time. If Ms. Samson replied, Chance didn't hear her.

The butterfly bush had finally earned its name. It was covered in beautiful, beautiful butterflies. Painted Ladies. They were orangey and black with white spots and long, delicate feelers. Chance stood for a long time and stared.

"Does your family know you're here?" Ms. Samson asked, when he looked up.

Chance shook his head. She stood. "I'll walk you home when I get back," she said, and left the room.

Chance's chair had not been stacked, so he fetched Matilda and went to his desk. Sitting down, he lifted the container, peered through the side and gasped. Matilda was dangling from the lid.

With great care, he snapped the lid off and lifted it to look more closely. She hung, moving a bit, from a little ball of thread that Chance knew was her silk. Matilda had attached.

"All right, Chance. Time to go. Angie was certainly glad to hear that you're safe. Mark arrived and looked for you and ..." Ms. Samson was talking as she entered the room. But she stopped when she saw what Chance was doing.

"She attached," Chance said.

"Oh," Ms. Samson said. "I'm so glad! On Friday morning she'll be ready to join the others on the butterfly bush."

Then Ms. Samson and Chance left the school together.

Chapter Eighteen

It was a long week for Chance. He knew he would have to wait seven days or so for Matilda to transform herself. But by Friday, about half the other chrysalides had cracked open and released brand-new butterflies into the world.

The classroom was aflutter, with butterflies and with excited children. Chance was excited some of the time, but he worried too. After all, he had buried the dead chrysalis. He knew what could happen. And Matilda wasn't really changing in there. At least, not that he could see.

Then another thought occurred to him.

If Matilda didn't die, if she transformed the way she was supposed to, she would be released. She would fly away into the world with all the rest of the butterflies. Chance knew that he should be happy about that. But he wasn't.

He stopped working on his storyboard. And when Ms. Samson asked him if he wanted to skip Learning Assistance on Friday afternoon to join the class in releasing the butterflies, he said no. He noted that Ken wasn't going to get to go either. For some reason or other, his father was picking him up at noon.

When Mrs. Johnson, his LA teacher, pulled out a story to read to her small Friday-afternoon group, Chance used Ralph's line. "We've heard that one a million times," he grumbled. Mrs. Johnson read it anyway, but she stopped four times to ask Chance to keep his hands and feet to himself.

Afterward, she gave them paper and pencils and asked them to draw a picture and write a word or two about the story. Chance grabbed the first pencil and deliberately snapped the tip off, ripping a hole in his paper and making a mark on the table. Mrs. Johnson gave him a new pencil and a fresh sheet of paper. Chance did it again.

"You'd better go back to class," Mrs. Johnson said, in a calm, even voice.

"I can't go back. They're not there," Chance shot back.

So he spent the last twenty minutes of Learning Assistance sitting at the other table with no pencils or paper — or anything else, for that matter — within reach.

Back in class, the kids seemed like volcanoes. Excitement erupted from them like molten lava. Chance did his best to ignore them, but he was their audience of one. They refused to leave him alone.

"You should have seen them, Chance," Ralph shouted across the room.

"Yeah," said Martha, just loud enough for him to hear. "You really should have come instead of staying behind sulking like a baby."

The shove he gave her then felt very controlled to Chance. He mouthed "Shut up!" at her at the same time, feeling the words on his teeth. Martha did not shut up, nor was Ms. Samson impressed with his self-control. Chance was kept after school once again. But Mrs. Laurence was not called in. To his great relief, he was not suspended.

"Can you see her wings yet?" Mark asked after school. He hadn't been allowed in the classroom because Chance was in trouble.

"Shut up!" Chance yelled back. "Can't you just shut up?" He felt the words deeper this time, in his chest.

Mark shrugged his shoulders. "Walk by yourself, then," he said bluntly, and took off for the park.

Then it was the weekend.

When Chance got out of bed on Saturday morning and pulled back the dark curtain, light streamed into the room. The trees were swaying violently in the wind, but the sky was brilliant blue. Chance hoped that the butterflies weren't having trouble in that wind.

Now it was the weekend, windy, bright, fresh Saturday. Matilda was locked up in the school and inside her own unchanging skin. Mark was mad at him again. And Angie and Doug were planning to drag him and Mark and Louise to some faraway park at the beach for the day. He had almost been pleased when they mentioned it. After all, he had hardly ever been to the beach.

Chance got himself dressed in runners, jeans and a sweatshirt. Then he slumped on his unmade bed, feet sticking out over the floor, and let his head clunk back against the wall. He could hear footsteps and muffled talk; Louise cried once for a minute or two. He could smell cooking. Probably pancakes and bacon, he thought. He loved pancakes and bacon. But not today. He lifted his head from the wall and let it clunk back once more.

Without a single word or knock of warning, his door opened.

"Get a move on, el creepo. My mom wants you down for breakfast, now."

Chance let the words, especially the "my

mom," glance off. He didn't even blink until Mark was gone. Then he wiggled forward until his feet met the floor, heaved himself to his feet and began the long, slow journey to the kitchen table.

* * *

It was a good thing that Louise's car seat was in the middle, between Mark and Chance. Angie and Doug tried to make conversation at first, but soon Angie gave up and put the radio on. Chance kept his face glued to the window the whole way, almost an hour, to the beach.

The last few blocks went slowly. Every light was red and the whole city seemed to be out and about. Streams of pedestrians crossed at every corner, all headed, Chance figured, for the water. Then Doug saw a parking spot and the drive was over.

"We'll walk from here," he said. "The lots at the beach are probably jammed."

"It's not summer," Mark said. "What are all these people doing here?"

"Same as us, I guess," Angie said.

Louise was perched high on Doug's back, and the picnic things and blanket were divided up between the rest of them. Chance hefted his bundle silently and off they trudged. It was hard to stay grumpy amid the throng, though. Everyone was smiling and chattering away. Was it just the weather, Chance wondered?

Finally, they crossed the last street and found themselves in an avenue of enormous trees, staring ahead at the water, rough, whitecapped. Both boys took off at a run.

"We'll see you at the water," Doug shouted, waving them on.

At the edge of the sand, they dumped their bundles and scuffed off their shoes. The sand was cold and sharp, more gravel than anything else, but they didn't care. Moments later they were standing on the hard, flat surface at the water's edge. Gulping salty air, they looked at each other and grinned. Then they turned back to the water just in time to shout a late warning to one another. They stumbled backward, but waves were already swirling around their feet and licking at their calves.

"It's a good thing I brought towels," Angie said, laughing, when Mark and Chance joined them at the top of the beach.

Shoes back on over sandy feet, Mark and Chance took off again, this time along the walkway beside the sand. Every kind of person imaginable shared the path with them: all ages, all sizes, all styles of dress, using every non-motorized form of transport known to humankind. They passed a concession stand, wishing in vain for a few dollars for fries or ice cream, stopped to watch beach volleyball for a while and then meandered on. They came to a basketball court and stopped, transfixed. This was the real thing. The players were good, really good. And they were tall, way taller than they looked on TV.

"I'll bet there're some NBA players out there," Mark said.

Chance nodded. He was impressed, but he wanted to go on. Most people seemed to be walking in the same direction he and

Mark had been. They were going somewhere; he could tell.

"Let's watch on the way back," he suggested.

"I want to hang out here. You go on ahead if you like. Pick me up on your way back."

Chance stood still, wanting to go but knowing he shouldn't.

"Oh, come on, kid. Mom and Dad don't need to know. There are lots of kids around. Just blend in."

So Chance did. He walked on, part of the happy crowd. He looked around at all the families, all the mothers and fathers and children on family outings. Well, he thought to himself, he was on a family outing too, wasn't he? Wasn't he?

He came round a bend and all such thoughts tumbled out of his head. Kites. That was what everyone was here to see. Kites. He had come upon a huge sloping green field, water on two sides, open to the wind. The field was filled with busy people. And the sky was filled with kites. Kites, twirling, twisting and dancing in the wind. Kites in all shapes. Kites in all colors. He saw dragons, box-shaped kites, winged kites and butterfly kites. On his right, a man was flying a matched pair, doing a dance in perfect unison. They made a whizzing sound like race cars on the track.

Chance walked slowly around the field, gazing upward. Sometimes he tried to trace a kite down to its owner on the ground. Not always easy. About halfway around he stopped to watch a small kite that stood apart from the others. It was orange and red and green, with a brilliant yellow tail, but its colors blurred together because of the speed and intricacy of its dance. Chance found himself hoping that Matilda would fly like that one day soon — better than that because she would not be constrained by a string. He smiled and began to work his way down from the little kite, searching for the skilled person who could make it dance in such glory. He found himself staring at Ken.

Chance's first impulse was to step forward, to call out a greeting. His second

was to back away, to stay out of sight. He did neither. He stayed where he was and watched. Ken controlled the string and ran at the same time, every part of him connected with that brilliant diamond in the sky. At one point he shouted, and Chance saw that the man who had picked Ken up at lunch yesterday was flying one of the matched sets. Ken's father. The man grinned and shouted back. Was it for this that Ken had left early yesterday?

Now Ken was coming to a stop, staring up at his kite, trying some new move, Chance thought. He was close by, just across the path. Chance stepped forward.

"Ken," he called loudly. Ken looked, but he seemed to look beyond Chance, at something behind him. Chance half turned, in time to see Angie running toward him, full tilt.

"Chance, there you are, thank God," Angie was saying as she ran the last few feet and folded him into her arms.

Chance squirmed, annoyed. There was Mark, standing behind her. He looked annoyed too. Chance looked back toward Ken just in time to see Ken's kite plummet to the ground, tangled with a big kite shaped like a fish. Ken's face was twisted in anger.

"You!" he yelled. "You made me do this. You make trouble at school. And now here ..."

"I'm sorry," Chance said, freeing himself from Angie's grasp. "I didn't mean to do that. I ... Your kite is so beautiful! And you're amazing! You made it dance!"

But Ken didn't seem to hear. He was running to where his kite had hit the ground, running to protect it from all the trampling feet.

Chance watched for a moment more. Then he turned to face Angie. Yes, he knew it was dangerous to go off alone. Yes, he understood that he was too far away, that it wasn't safe, an eight-year-old all alone among all these people. But while he nodded his head or mumbled yes, over and over, he would not have missed seeing those kites for anything. He would talk to Ken again on Monday; Ken would have to understand.

Chapter Nineteen

On Monday morning, five more butterflies had come into the world. But Chance barely glanced at them, so intent was he on his own special chrysalis. As he stared, a warm glow started in his belly and spread to his chest. Tears pricked at his eyes. Friday's white, dead-looking skin was now almost see-through. And through it he could see the hint of a wing, a delicate black and orange wing.

Chance danced to his desk, dragging his chair to the loud complaints of his classmates. He didn't care about a thing, until he faced Ken. Ken looked at him for a moment, his eyes ice. Then he turned back to his work. As the day passed, Chance tried to catch Ken's eye again, to find an opportunity to apologize, to tell him one more time how amazing his flying had been. But Ken never once let that happen.

On Tuesday morning, Ms. Samson announced that they would be releasing the rest of the butterflies before lunch. "Mr. Redding's class are releasing their butterflies first thing," she said, "so all the butterflies can go out into the world together."

"What about the last one?" Chance called out. "She's still in her chrysalis."

"Yes," Ms. Samson said, "that's all right, Chance. We'll release her when she's ready."

Chance had a lot on his mind when he went out for recess. But all his worries turned to horror when he rounded the school and took in the scene before him. At first it seemed like nothing. Just two boys playing some sort of throwing game with rocks against the side of the school. Then he saw what they were aiming at. One of Mr. Redding's butterflies was perched high on the wall. Those boys were trying to kill it!

"You stop," Chance screamed, shooting toward them at the same time.

The boys were bigger than he was, and they were mad. This little third-grader was turning a little game into a big deal. But other kids were wandering over and they didn't really want Chance spouting off. The taller one gave him a shove and the grunted order, "Beat it, kid." And that was the end of it. They jogged away toward the soccer field, brushing aside questions on the way.

Chance almost went after them. He even thought about finding a supervisor, which would have been the first time Chance had actually looked for an adult's help. But he was winded and he knew he didn't stand much of a chance with those kids. Besides, he had saved the butterfly.

A new worry occurred to him as he made his way back to the primary end of the grounds. What would stop those boys from going after his class's butterflies at lunchtime?

Back in class, an hour remained before they were to release the butterflies. Chance wanted to save them, but he didn't know how. He put up his hand and told the class about the two boys. Ms. Samson was horrified, but she said that they would release them over by the woods, so they wouldn't be around the school at lunchtime. But Chance knew it wasn't that simple. Butterflies would fly where they liked. And insects didn't understand about danger from humans. Could they take them somewhere else for their release? No, Ms. Samson said. She was sure that it would be all right.

Then they did a times-tables drill. Chance got every one wrong, except the ones. He even missed the zeros, and he usually knew those.

At twenty past eleven, Ms. Samson lined up the class in pairs. Chance stayed at his desk.

"I'm telling you, you can't do this!" he said, giving it one more try.

"That's enough, Chance. We all know how you feel," Ms. Samson said. "Now come join us."

"I'm not taking one. I won't."

"That's just fine. There aren't enough to go around anyway."

But as it turned out, several children were away that day. There were enough butterflies for one per pair. Ken stood alone at the end of the line. Chance made his way as slowly as he could to take up a position a few feet behind Ken. Ken gave him an angry look, making it clear that he did not want Chance for a partner anyway. Chance took another step back.

Ms. Samson caught each butterfly gently in a paper cup, put her hand over the top and then transferred the cup to a waiting pair of children. The pairs argued over who should get to hold it, until she said that they would take turns. The holder would give the cup to his or her partner on the other side of the adventure playground. Then each pair would hold the cup together during the release. The squabbling died down.

When Ken took his cup, Chance watched, almost wishing that he was up there with him. But Ken did not look back once. He held the cup with great care and followed the class outside. Chance held back a bit, but the first pair was holding the outside door open. They yelled at him to hurry up. So he walked outside into the bright sun. He thought of butterflies lit up by that sun, easy to spot. Easy to crush with rocks.

It was wrong. He knew it was wrong, and he had told. Chance was not going to watch the butterflies being released to certain death. Instead, he lowered himself into the tire swing, pushing off with his foot so that the swing moved gently. He lay back, stared up past the chain and the wooden structure at the blue, blue sky. He conjured kites instead of butterflies. And he actually saw a beautiful blue bird with a pointy beak. It flew right overhead.

Then, "Chance, we're all waiting for you. What are you doing here? You think the butterflies like sitting inside cups while we search for you?" Martha and Preeti stared down at him, their whining, angry voices blended.

Chance thought about ignoring them or crashing the swing into them, but Preeti was holding that precious cup, so he pulled himself up and out and followed them down to the field.

Ms. Samson had kept her word. Everyone was standing against the chain-link fence over by the woods. They looked mad. Chance thought of the butterflies in those cups, airless, hot, jostling more and more as the children grew impatient. He picked up his pace.

"Okay, okay, let them go! What are you waiting for me for?" he shouted.

And that did it. The class did not wait for Ms. Samson's word. Four hands gripped each cup and together thrust it upward. Several butterflies took to the air and Chance felt a surge of relief. But there were ten butterflies to release. Children were shaking their cups, turning them upside down, reaching inside to give the butterflies a nudge. Chance wanted to run away, but moved closer instead.

One pair had tipped their butterfly onto the ground, where it sat, unmoving. They shouted and danced around the delicate creature, but to no avail. Chance's heart stopped. Any second a butterfly was going to be stamped to death or crushed between eager fingers.

Then, finally, Ms. Samson blew the whistle. She blew the whistle and they all did exactly what they always did when they heard that sound outside. They froze. Within seconds she had them sitting down on the grass, being sure not to sit on any butterflies, and waiting and watching for the butterflies to take flight.

"Let them take their time," she said. "Watch what they do!"

Chance had sat down too when she said that. He found himself near Ken once again. So he watched what Ken was doing. He did not think that Ken had taken part in all the mayhem before. Now, Ken held the cup carefully tipped into the palm of his other hand. As Chance watched, holding his breath, the butterfly crept out onto Ken's palm. It rested there a moment, then took flight. Together, Chance and Ken tipped back their heads and watched that flight.

Even though they were looking right up into the sky, they had no warning. Just a flash of blue, and the butterfly was gone. The bird, the beautiful, blue bird with the sharp beak, had eaten Ken's butterfly.

In one breath, Chance and Ken gasped. They kept staring into the sky until the bird was gone. Then they turned and stared at each other. Ken did not speak, though. He turned back, and hunched himself up with his arms around his legs and his face on his knees until Ms. Samson asked them to line up to go back in.

Chance wanted to tell her what had happened to Ken's butterfly, but it was already lunchtime by the time they got back to class. The lunch monitors were waiting for them, and Ms. Samson disappeared to the staff room right away.

He had taken his lunch to his desk along with the rest of the class, but he had no interest in eating it. He looked over to see what Ken was up to. He wasn't at his desk. Chance was sure he had come back. He had been right in front of Chance walking into the classroom. There he was, at the butterfly bush. He was staring at something. But all the butterflies were gone.

Then Chance understood. Quietly, avoiding the lunch monitors' attention and holding his breath to hang onto his hope, he rose from his desk, made his way to the back of the room and across to stand beside Ken. Yes! Matilda's shell, her chrysalis, was cracked open and empty. Right beside it, hanging by delicate legs from the branch, was a brand-new butterfly. Her wings were small and crinkly, but she was wonderful. Chance knew that she had to hang like that for a while so her wings could fill up with liquid and expand. Then they would dry and she would be able to use them.

He looked at Ken and grinned. Then his face fell.

"I'm sorry that the bird ate your butterfly," he said. "And I'm sorry I made your kite fall on Saturday."

Ken looked at him for a long moment before he spoke.

"I do not think you meant to make my kite fall." He paused. "You did not touch my kite. I made it fall. I was not taking care."

Then they turned their attention back to Matilda. But not for long.

"What are you two doing over there?" Lori-Mae was on to them. "Get back to your desks and eat your lunch!"

"But this butterfly …" Chance started.

"You heard her," Harmenjeet snapped. "It's been nothing but butterflies and caterpillars in this class for weeks. Now, get back to your desks!"

Ken had already gone. Chance followed. But he did not eat his lunch. He waited until Harmenjeet and Lori-Mae were deep in conversation again. Then he slipped back to watch Matilda.

She wasn't there. He had only been gone a moment, but now she was not there. The branch beside her empty shell was bare. Chance found her soon enough.

Matilda had fallen. She was lying on the table on her side, quivering slightly. One of her wings was caught underneath her. That wing would be stunted if she stayed there. Then she would die.

Chance didn't have much faith in the lunch monitors, but they were all he had at the moment. They did come when he called them, although they wondered what he was doing back over there again.

"It'll probably be all right," Harmenjeet said.

"Yeah, and what can you do anyway?" Lori-Mae added.

Then they turned their attention back to the class, who wanted to know what was going on. "Just stay put, all of you. You gotta stay put till the bell goes."

But Ken didn't listen. He got up to put his lunch bag away and on the way back joined Chance at the bush. Chance had noticed before that the monitors were never as hard on Ken as they were on everyone else, because they had been told so many times that he didn't understand English.

"We must save her," Ken said.

"Yes," Chance answered. He had been

working on an idea. If he could just bring the branch down to Matilda, maybe she could grab on with her clingy little feet. After all, that was what she had been doing before she fell.

He searched the room. What could he use for a branch? His gaze fell on the yogurt container of paintbrushes beside the sink. Perfect.

Holding the brush end in his hand, he reached under the netting. He held the long handle right over Matilda's legs, right down, pretty much touching. Just as he had hoped, she reached up with her feet and grabbed hold.

He lifted the brush carefully, slowly. Ken was silent beside him.

But something went wrong. Matilda fell. She just let go and fell. She couldn't hold on. Ken gasped. Chance choked back tears. Then he stood up stiffly, pulled his shoulders back and set himself to try again.

"This time it will work," Ken whispered.

Chance brought the paintbrush down to Matilda again. Ken was gripping the table edge. Chance guessed that Ken was wishing right along with him. Wishing, "Please, Matilda, please hold on and don't let go."

Chance lifted the brush so slowly it hardly seemed to move. Matilda held on with her delicate feet, held on all the way. And Chance laid the brush as gently as he could across the edge of the bucket that held the bush. That way Matilda could just stay there until she was ready to fly.

Where she had lain on the table there were little drops of red. When there had been red on the table before, some kids started jumping around and calling out that that was blood. That the butterflies were dying.

But Chance knew what it was and what it meant. They all knew, really. It wasn't blood. It was the liquid butterflies use to pump up their wings. Maconium, it was called. The extra drips out. It means the butterfly is really living, getting ready to fly. Not dying at all!

Chapter Twenty

Chance was watching Matilda when the bell rang at the end of lunch. He had no intention of going outside. Ken had gone off obediently right after the bell.

The lunch monitors were annoyed. They had already put Chance's name on the board to let Ms. Samson know he was being uncooperative. Now they just wanted him out so that they could leave.

"Out, Chance," Lori-Mae said fiercely. "We're not going to stay around here waiting for you."

"Then leave," he spat out. "I don't care. I have to stay here."

"Let's take him to the office," Harmenjeet said.

"But he won't go," Lori-Mae responded. "He's just going to sit there."

"I'll carry him if I have to," Harmenjeet snapped. "We're supposed to meet everybody outside."

Chance had a sinking feeling that she meant what she said. He watched her approach. She looked determined.

"I'm not going to the office," he said, darting past her and out the door, coat forgotten.

He hadn't wanted to leave Matilda, even though he was pretty sure she would be all right now. But he was also afraid of what he would find outside.

There could be killing going on out there. Just like at recess. Only now there were so many more butterflies to kill. If he saw one kid holding a stone, or raising a foot to stamp a fragile red and black wing, he was going to turn into the Terminator. That kid would never throw or stamp again.

Chance searched the schoolyard, looking

for children on the attack. He searched the ground beneath his feet for shreds of wings, for broken bodies.

He found nothing.

The butterflies that had struggled to get off the ground an hour before were gone. They must have managed to fly. They must be safe. Chance's heart started to lift. And as his heart lifted, he looked up to the sky.

And as he stopped listening for sounds of hatred, he heard sounds of joy.

A group of children on the grass field were pointing up and calling, "Look, look!"

Chance followed their gaze. High in the sky, well out of reach of any child, two colorful spots fluttered against the deep blue.

Two Painted Lady butterflies had stayed behind long enough to say goodbye.

Chance stood for a long, long time staring up into the sky. When he looked down, he noticed Mark up the hill on the soccer field. He had stopped playing and was looking up too. While Chance watched, Mark raised his hand in a sort of salute to the butterflies. Chance glanced once more up into the sky, then he took off at a run for the playground past the soccer field.

When he got close to Mark, he slowed down and gestured upward.

"You saw them, huh?" he called out.

"Yeah," Mark answered. "I saw them."

Chapter Twenty-One

After lunch, Chance counted the minutes. He knew it took about half an hour for the wings to extend fully and then another half-hour for them to dry. He figured that Matilda's wings should be dry by now, but he wanted to be sure to give her enough time. He wanted to be sure that she was ready. He had decided that she needed one more hour.

It was time for shared reading. Chance had no hope of concentrating on a book, but he looked over at Ken, who was reading alone again. Ken had partners assigned to him for every day, but if Ms. Samson wasn't paying attention, sometimes they went and read with someone else.

"Want to be partners?" Chance asked.

"Yes," Ken answered.

It was that easy.

They ended up talking about Matilda.

After shared reading, they worked on their storyboards. Chance had no trouble working on his today. The story was happening right in the room while he was making pictures to go with it. But he left the last square of the paper blank. It might be unlucky to fill it in before it had actually happened.

Finally, he was sure that an hour had passed since lunch. Ken confirmed it.

"Will you help me release the last butterfly?" Chance said.

Ken's face lit up. "Let's go!"

Together they approached Ms. Samson.

"I want to let the butterfly go now," Chance said.

"Yes," she said quietly back to him.

"Can Ken help?" he asked.

"Of course," Ms. Samson said.

While she got the Styrofoam cup ready,

Chance and Ken watched Matilda. She perched on a branch, perfectly still, but Chance knew she longed to fly. And not just to another branch, but far away. He stood and watched her and waited for Ms. Samson.

Just as she had done earlier in the day with the other butterflies, Ms. Samson reached under the netting and gently put the cup over Matilda. Then she slid her hand over the top of the cup, holding the insect safe inside. When she had the cup outside the netting, Chance held out his hands. She let him take the cup and slide his palm over the top in place of hers.

He turned to Ken and held out the cup, but Ken shook his head.

"It is your turn," he said.

Together they slipped out of the classroom, leaving behind the happy chaos of children drawing and writing and talking. The hallway was peaceful. Immediately to the right was the outside door. Ms. Samson pushed it open and let the two boys pass.

"I'll wait for you here," she said. "Stay in sight."

Chance moved away from the shade of the school into the brilliant sunlight. He turned and looked at Ken, who gestured upward.

After that, Chance did not hesitate. He took his hand from the top of the cup and looked inside at his butterfly. Then he grasped the cup with both hands and thrust it up into the air.

"Be free, butterfly," he said.

And all the sadness and loneliness of the morning washed away as he watched her, not his butterfly anymore, take to the sky. For a rare moment he stood absolutely still, as Matilda fluttered far above him against the blue. Then she vanished behind the school.

"She's free now," he said to Ken and Ms. Samson as they re-entered the school.

"Yes," they replied together.

* * *

Back at his desk, Chance sifted through his pencil crayons. To do Matilda justice

he was going to need the bluest blue and the brightest orange.

* * *

Mark was a few minutes late picking Chance up that afternoon. When he arrived, the classroom was deserted except for Chance and Ms. Samson, packing away the butterfly bush. Mark stepped into the room.

"What happened?" he asked.

Chance stopped stuffing the netting into a bag and looked up, his face radiant.

"She's free, Mark," he said. "Matilda's a butterfly now. She's free."

Mark's whole body relaxed. He grinned.

"Hey, that's great news," he said. Then, "Come on, Chance. It's time to go home."

Orca Young Reader Series

Hoop Crazy! *(Eric Walters)*
A nerd joins Nick and Kia's team.
1-55143-184-X • $6.95 CAN; $4.99 USA

Full Court Press *(Eric Walters)*
Nick and Kia try out for the school team.
1-55143-169-6 • $6.95 CAN; $4.99 USA

Three on Three *(Eric Walters)*
Winning the basketball tournament is going to be tough,
but making a new friend is tougher.
1-55143-170-X • $6.95 CAN; $4.99 USA

The Freezing Moon *(Becky Citra)*
Can Ellie overcome her fears and protect her brother
when Papa disappears in a storm? The sequel to *Ellie's
New Home*.
1-55143-181-5 • $6.95 CAN; $4.99 USA

Ellie's New Home *(Becky Citra)*
In 1835, a young girl and her brother are left with
strangers while their father goes ahead to find land and
build a homestead.
1-55143-164-5 • $6.95 CAN; $4.99 USA

Daughter of Light *(martha attema)*
In the darkest days of WWII, nine-year-old Ria is determined that her mother will give birth in a home filled with light.
1-55143-179-3 • $6.95 CAN; $4.99 USA

The Keeper and the Crows *(Andrea Spalding)*
A smart thriller that introduces the themes of The Quest and the timeless struggle of good over evil.
1-55143-141-X • $6.95 CAN; $4.99 USA

Jesse's Star *(Ellen Schwartz)*
A compelling history of one family's struggle to be free in the new world.
1-55143-143-2 • $6.95 CAN; $4.99 USA

Phoebe and the Gypsy *(Andrea Spalding)*
A chance meeting with a gypsy fortune teller helps a young girl understand and control her gift of second sight.
1-55143-135-1 • $6.95 CAN; $4.99 USA

Maggie de Vries is the author of the picture book *Once Upon a Golden Apple* (Penguin, 1991), written with Jean Little and illustrated by Phoebe Gilman. Her upcoming picture book *How Sleep Found Tabitha* (Orca), illustrated by Sheena Lott, will be released in 2002. Maggie de Vries is a writer, editor and teacher who divides her time between Vancouver and Victoria, BC.